Books by Margaret Millar

The Devil Loves Me
The Weak-Eyed Bat
The Invisible Worm
Wall of Eyes
Fire Will Freeze
The Iron Gates
Experiment in Springtime
It's All in the Family
The Cannibal Heart
Do Evil in Return
Vanish in an Instant
Rose's Last Summer
Wives and Lovers
Beast in View
An Air That Kills
The Listening Walls
A Stranger in My Grave
How Like an Angel
The Fiend
The Birds and the Beasts Were There
Beyond This Point Are Monsters

*BEYOND
THIS
POINT
ARE
MONSTERS*

Margaret Millar

RANDOM HOUSE   NEW YORK

BEYOND THIS POINT ARE MONSTERS

FOR JUDGE
JOHN A. WESTWICK

*BEYOND
THIS
POINT
ARE
MONSTERS*

CHAPTER
ONE

IN DEVON'S DREAM they were searching the reservoir again for Robert. It was almost the way it had happened the first time, with the Mexican policeman, Valenzuela, shouting orders to his men, and the young divers standing around in rubber suits with aqualungs strapped to their backs.

In the dream Devon watched, mute and helpless, from the ranch house. The real Devon had gone out to protest to Estivar, the foreman: "Why are they looking for him in there?" "They have to look every place, Mrs. Osborne."

"The water's so dirty. Robert's a very clean person." "Yes, ma'am." "He would never have gone in such dirty water." "He might not have had much to say about it, ma'am."

The water, used only for irrigation, was too murky for the divers to work, and in the end the police used a giant scoop and strainer. They spent hours dragging the bottom. All they found were rusting pieces of machinery and old tires and pieces of lumber and the muddy bones of a newborn baby. Finding the nameless, faceless child had upset the policeman, Valenzuela, more than finding a dozen Roberts. It was as if the Roberts of this world always did something to deserve their fate, however bloody or wet or feverish. But the child, the baby— *"Goddam,"* Valenzuela said, crossing himself, and took the little pile of bones away in a shoe box.

She woke up to the sound of Dulzura knocking on the bedroom door.

"Mrs. Osborne? You awake?" The door opened no more than a crack. "You better get up now. Breakfast is on the stove."

"It's early," Devon said. "Only six-thirty."

"But this is the *day*. Have you forgot?"

"No." Not very likely. She'd signed the petition herself while the lawyer watched, looking relieved that she'd finally consented.

Dulzura's small fat hand trembled on the door. "I'm scared. Everybody will be staring at me."

"You only have to tell the truth."

"How am I sure of the truth after all this time? And if I lie after swearing on the Bible, Estivar says they'll put me in jail."

"He was joking."

"He didn't laugh."

"They won't put you in jail," Devon said. "I'll be ready for breakfast in ten minutes."

But she lay still, listening to Dulzura's leaden step on

the stairs and the grumbling of the wind as it went round and round the house trying to get in. The autumn night had been warm. Devon's short brown hair was moist and her nightgown clung damply to her body, as though she herself had been fished out of the reservoir and stretched on the bed to dry, a half-drowned mermaid.

Dulzura would tell the truth, of course, because it was too simple to distort: after dinner Robert had gone out to look for his dog and on the way he'd stopped in the kitchen to see Dulzura. He wished her a happy birthday, kidded her about getting to be a big girl and went out the back door toward the garage.

Robert's car was still there, the top down, the key in the ignition. Estivar said it was bad policy to leave the car like that, it was too much of a temptation to the Mexican migrant workers who came to harvest lemons in the spring and crate tomatoes in the summer and pick cantaloupe in the fall. Every group of migrants that had arrived and departed during the past year undoubtedly knew about the car, but no attempt had ever been made to steal it. Perhaps Estivar had warned them severely or perhaps they thought such a car would have a curse on it. Whatever the reason, it lay dead and undisturbed under its shroud of dust.

The tides of migrants that came and went were governed by the sun the way the ocean tides were governed by the moon. It was now October, the peak season of the year, and the bunkhouse was full. Devon had no personal connection with the migrant workers. They spoke no English, and Estivar discouraged her from trying to communicate with them in her high school Spanish. She didn't know their names or where they came from. Small and hungry, they moved across her fields like rodents. *"Must have been a couple of wetbacks,"* one of the deputies said. *"Must have robbed and killed him and buried him some place." "We have no wetbacks here,"* Estivar said sharply.

Later Estivar told Devon that the deputy was a very ignorant man because the term wetbacks, *mojados,* was applicable only in Texas where the U.S.–Mexican border was the Rio Grande River; here, in California, where the border was marked by miles of barbed-wire fence, the illegal entrants were properly called *alambres,* wires.

Devon got out of bed and went over to the window to pull aside the drapes. She had long since moved out of the bedroom she'd shared with Robert into the smallest room on the second floor of the ranch house. Small rooms were less lonely, easier to fill. This one, which faced south, had a sweeping view of the river valley, and in the distance the parched hills of Tijuana with its wooden shacks and its domed cathedral the same color as the mustard they sold for hot dogs at the race track and the bull ring. Tijuana looked best at night when it became a cluster of starry lights on the horizon, or at dawn when the cathedral dome turned pink and the shacks were still hidden by darkness.

Through the open window Devon could hear the phone ringing in the kitchen below and Dulzura answering it, her voice shrill as a parrot's because telephones made her nervous. A minute later she was at the bedroom door again, breathing heavily from exertion and resentment.

"It's his mother, says it's important."

"Tell her I'll call her back."

"She don't like to wait."

No, Devon thought, Robert's mother didn't like to wait. But she had waited, the same as the rest of them, for the sound of a doorbell, a phone, a car in the driveway, a step in the hall; she had waited for a letter, a telegram, a postcard, a message from a friend or a stranger.

"Tell her I'll call her back," Devon said.

From the window she could see, too, the rows of tamarisks planted to break the wind and protect the reservoir from blowing sand. To the east was the dry riverbed and to the west the fields of tomatoes, already harvested. The fields were alive with small birds. They swooped between the rows of plants, fluttered among the yellowing leaves, pecked at the rotting remains of fruit and searched the ground for fallen seeds and insects. Estivar could identify every one of them. He called them by their Mexican names, which made them all seem foreign and exotic to Devon until she found out that many of them were birds she'd known back home. The *chupamirto* was just a hummingbird, the *cardelina* a goldfinch, the *golondrina* a swallow.

Other things which had familiar names were not familiar at all. To Devon, born and brought up on the East Coast, rain was what spoiled a picnic or a trip to the zoo, not something people measured in tenths of inches like misers with molten gold. And a river had always been a permanent thing, like the Hudson or the Delaware or the Potomac. The river she watched now from her bedroom window was bone-dry most of the year, yet sometimes it turned into a rampaging torrent strong enough to carry a truck downstream. There were few bridges. It was generally assumed that when it rained hard, people would have sense enough to stay home or stick to the main highway; and when it was dry, they simply drove or walked across the riverbed as if it were a special road, untaxed and maintenance-free.

The far side of the river marked the boundary line of the next ranch, which belonged to Leo Bishop. When Robert brought her home as his bride a year and a half ago, Leo Bishop was the first neighbor she'd met. Robert asked her to be especially nice to him because he'd lost his wife suddenly and tragically during the winter. Devon had done her best, but there were still times when he seemed as foreign to her as any of the *alambres*.

Devon showered and began to dress. The clothes she was to wear had been hanging ready for a week. She had driven into San Diego to meet Robert's mother and Robert's mother had picked the outfit, a brown sharkskin suit a shade lighter than Devon's hair and a shade darker than her tanned skin. It made her look as though she and the suit had come out of the same dye vat, but she didn't argue with the choice. Brown seemed as good a color as any for a young woman about to become a widow on a sunny day in autumn.

She went down the back stairs that led directly into the kitchen.

Dulzura was at the stove, stirring something in a skillet with her left hand and fanning herself with her right. She was not yet thirty years old, but her youth, like the stool she sat on, was camouflaged by folds of fat.

She said, without looking around, "I'm making some scrambled eggs to go with the *chorizo.*"

"I'll just have orange juice and coffee, thanks."

"Mr. Osborne used to be crazy about *chorizo,* he had a real Mexican stomach... You should anyway try the eggs. See how nice they look."

Devon glanced briefly at the moist yellow mass rusted with chili powder and turned away. "They look very nice."

"But you don't like."

"Not this morning."

"No Mrs. Osborne, no little dog, I will have to eat everything myself. Obalz."

It was Dulzura's favorite expression and for a long time Devon had assumed it was a Spanish word indicating displeasure. She'd finally asked the foreman, Estivar, about it.

"There is no such word in my language," Estivar said.

"But it must mean something, Dulzura uses it all the time."

"Oh, it means something all right, you can bet on that."

"I see. It's English."

"Yes, ma'am."

Dulzura was one of Estivar's so-called cousins. He had

great numbers of them. If they spoke English, he claimed they were from the San Diego or Los Angeles branch of the family; if they spoke only Spanish, they were from the Sonora branch, or the Sinaloa or Jalisco or Chihuahua, whichever word suited his fancy if not the facts. At times of peak employment Estivar's cousins swarmed over the valley like an army of occupation. They planted, cultivated, irrigated; they pruned, thinned, stripped, sprayed; they picked, sorted, baled, boxed and bunched. Then suddenly they would disappear, as if the earth from which such an abundance of produce had been taken had absorbed the workers themselves like fertilizer.

Dulzura scraped the eggs out of the skillet into a bowl. "His mother on the phone, she said I better wear stockings. I only got the pair I'm saving for my brother's wedding."

"You can wear them more than once, surely."

"Not if I have to kneel when I swear on the Bible."

"Nobody kneels in a courtroom." Devon had never been in a courtroom but she spoke with conviction because she knew Dulzura was watching for any sign of uncertainty, her eyes dark and moist as ripe olives. "The women will be wearing stockings, and all the men coats and ties."

"Even Estivar and Mr. Bishop?"

"Yes."

The phone began ringing again and Devon went down the hall to answer on the extension in the study.

The study had been Robert's room. For a long time it had remained, like his car in the garage, exactly the way he left it. It was too painful for Devon to go inside or even to pass the closed door. Now the room was altered. As soon as the date for the hearing had been set, Devon began packing Robert's things in cardboard cartons, planning to store them in the attic—his tennis rackets and the trophies he'd won, his collection of silver coins, the maps of places he'd wanted to go, the books he'd intended to read.

Devon had cried so hard over the task that Dulzura began crying too, and they wailed together like a couple of old Irishwomen at a wake. After it was over and Devon could see again out of her swollen eyes, she took a marking pencil and printed Salvation Army on each of the cartons. Estivar was carrying the last of them into the front hall when Robert's mother arrived from the city, as she sometimes did, without warning.

Devon expected Mrs. Osborne to be disturbed by the sight of the cartons or at least to argue about their disposition. Instead, Mrs. Osborne calmly offered to deliver them to the Salvation Army herself. She even helped Estivar load the trunk of her car and the back seat. She was half a head taller than Estivar and almost as strong, and the two of them worked together quickly and efficiently and in silence as though they'd been partners on many such jobs in the past. Mrs. Osborne was seated behind the wheel ready to leave when she turned to Devon and said in her soft, firm voice: *"Robert always intended to clean up his study. He'll be glad we saved him the trouble."*

Devon closed the door of the study and picked up the phone. "Yes?"

"Why didn't you call me back, Devon?"

"There was no hurry. It's still very early."

"I'm well aware of it. I spent the night watching the clock."

"I'm sorry you couldn't sleep."

"I didn't want to," Mrs. Osborne said. "I was trying to reason things out, to decide whether this is the right step to take."

"We must take it. Mr. Ford and the other lawyers told you that."

"I don't necessarily have to believe what people tell me."

"Mr. Ford is an expert."

"On legal matters, yes. But where Robert is concerned, *I* am the expert. And what you're going to do today is wrong. You should have refused to sign the papers. Perhaps it's still not too late. You could call Ford and ask him to arrange a postponement because you need more time to think."

"I've had a whole year to think. Nothing has changed."

"But it could, it might. Any day now the phone might ring or there'll be a knock at the door and there he'll be, good as new. Maybe he was kidnapped and is being held captive somewhere across the border. Or he had a blow on the head the night he disappeared and he's suffering from amnesia. Or—"

Devon held the telephone away from her ear. She didn't want to hear any more of the *maybes* Mrs. Osborne had dreamed up during the long nights and elaborated on during the long days.

"Devon? *Devon.*" It was the closest thing to a scream Mrs. Osborne ever permitted herself except when she was alone. "Are you listening to me?"

"The hearing will be held today. I can't stop it now and wouldn't if I could."

"But what if—"

"There isn't going to be a knocking at the door or a ringing of the phone. There isn't going to be anything."

"It's cruel, Devon, it's cruel to destroy someone's hope like this."

"It would be crueler to encourage you to wait for something that can't happen."

"Can't? That's a strong word. Even Ford doesn't say can't. Miracles are happening every day. Look at the organ transplants they're doing all over the country. Suppose Robert was found dying and they gave his heart to someone else. That would be better than nothing, wouldn't it? —knowing his heart was alive—wouldn't it?"

Mrs. Osborne went on, repeating the same things she'd

11 /

been saying throughout the year, not even bothering any more to make it seem new by altering a word here, a phrase there.

Two clocks at opposite ends of the house began sounding the hour: the grandfather clock in the living room, and in the kitchen the cuckoo clock Dulzura kept on the wall above the stove. Dulzura claimed it was a present from her husband, but nobody believed she ever had a husband, let alone one that gave her presents. The grandfather clock belonged to Mrs. Osborne. Carved at the base were the words meant to accompany its chimes:

God Is With You,
Doubt Him Never,
While The Hours
Leave Forever.

When Mrs. Osborne moved out of the ranch house to let Devon and Robert occupy it alone, she'd taken along her antique cherrywood desk and mahogany piano, her silver tea service and collection of English bone china, but she left the clock behind. She no longer believed that God was with her and she didn't want to be reminded that the hours left forever.

Seven o'clock.

The Mexican workers were coming out of the bunkhouse and out of the old wooden building, formerly a barn, that was now equipped as a mess hall. Quickly and quietly they piled into the back of the big truck that would drop them off in whatever fields were ready for harvesting. There was little in their lives except hard work, and the food that made work possible.

At noon they would sit in the bleachers built by Estivar's sons beside the reservoir and eat their lunch in the shade of the tamarisks. At five they would have tortillas and beans in the mess hall and by nine-thirty all the bunkhouse lights would be out. The hours that left forever were good riddance.

Agnes Osborne was still talking. Between the time Devon had stopped listening and the time she started again, Mrs. Osborne had somehow reconciled herself to the fact that the hearing would be held as scheduled, beginning at ten o'clock. "It will probably be better if we met right in the courtroom so we won't miss each other. Do you remember the number?"

"Five."

"Will you be bringing your own car into town?"

"Leo Bishop asked me to ride with him."

"And you accepted?"

"Yes."

"You'd better call and tell him you've changed your mind. Today of all days you don't want to start people gossiping about you and Leo."

"There's nothing to gossip about."

"If you're too nervous to drive yourself, come with Estivar in the station wagon. Oh, and make sure Dulzura wears hose, will you?"

"Why? Dulzura's not on trial. We're not on trial."

"Don't be naïve," Mrs. Osborne said harshly. "Of course we're on trial, all of us. Ford tried to keep everything as quiet as possible, naturally, but witnesses had to be subpoenaed and many people had to be given legal notice of the time and place of the hearing, so it's not exactly a secret. It won't be exactly a picnic, either. Signing a piece of paper is one thing, it's quite another to get up in a courtroom and relive those terrible days in public. But it's your decision, you're Robert's wife."

"I'm not his wife," Devon said. "I'm his widow."

CHAPTER
TWO

THE TWO CARS moved slowly along the dirt road, the dust rising in the air behind them like smoke signals.

In the lead was the station wagon driven by Estivar. He was nearly fifty now, but his hair was still dark and thick, and from a distance his quick wiry body looked like a boy's. He had dressed for the occasion in the only suit he possessed, a dark blue gabardine which he kept for the yearly banquets of the Agricultural Association and for his appearances before the immigration authorities when some of his men were picked up by the border patrol for having entered the country illegally.

The blue suit, which was intended to make him appear respectable and, hopefully, beyond reproach, merely emphasized his uneasiness, his mistrust of this latest turn of events. If there was to be official recognition of Robert Osborne's death, it should take place not in court but in church, with prayers and pleadings and long somber words intoned by gray-faced priests.

Estivar had brought his wife, Ysobel, with him for moral support and because she refused to stay home. She was a *mestiza,* half-Indian, with high red-bronze cheekbones and flat black eyes that looked blind and missed nothing. She held her neck rigid and her body erect, refusing to surrender to the motion of the car.

In the seat behind Ysobel, Dulzura sat sideways and stretched her legs out straight in front of her in order to save her stockings at the knees. She wore a giant of a dress, with dwarf horses galloping around the hem and across the pockets. She'd purchased the dress for a weekend trip to the races in Agua Caliente, but the man who proposed the trip failed to show up. The only time Dulzura felt bitter about his defection was when she thought of the money she might have won.

"Five hundred pesos, maybe," she said aloud to no one in particular. "That's forty dollars."

Beside Dulzura sat Lum Wing, the elderly Chinese who cooked for the men. He never associated with them, he merely arrived when they did, carrying a bag with his clothes in it and a padlocked wooden case containing his collection of knives, his whetstone sharpener and a chess set; and when the men left, he left, but not with them or even in the same direction if he could help it.

Lum Wing sucked on the stem of an unlit corncob pipe, wondering what exactly was expected of him. A man in uniform had handed him a piece of paper and told him he'd better show up, by God, or else. He had a premonition, based on some facts he thought no one else knew, that he would end up in jail. And when a good cook landed in jail, no one was ever in a hurry to set him free, that much he'd learned from experience. Out of nervousness he'd been swallowing air all morning and every now and then the excess would escape in a long loud burp.

Ysobel spoke to her husband in Spanish. "Tell him to stop making those disgusting noises."

"He can't help it."

"Do you suppose he's sick?"

"No."

"It seems to me he looks more yellow than the last time I saw him. Perhaps it's contagious. I'm beginning not to feel so well myself."

"Me too," Dulzura said. "I think we should stop off at a place in Boca de Rio and have something to steady our nerves."

"You know what she means by something. Not coffee, I can tell you. And wouldn't it look splendid to have us walk into the courthouse with her reeling drunk."

Estivar braked the car sharply and ordered them both to keep quiet, and the journey continued for a while in silence. Past the lemon groves sweet with the scent of blossoms, past the acres of stubble where the alfalfa had been cut, and the field of ripening pumpkins which Estivar's youngest son, Jaime, had grown to take into Boca de Rio for Halloween jack-o'-lanterns and Thanksgiving pies.

Jaime was fourteen. He lay now on his stomach in the back of the station wagon, gnawing his right thumbnail and wondering if the kids at school knew where he was and what he had to do. Maybe they were already blowing it up into something wild like he was a friend of the fuzz. Word like that could put a guy down for the rest of his life.

It was the pumpkins that had done it to him. During the last week in October he had delivered some of them to school for the fair and the rest to a grocery store in Boca de Rio. The following Saturday Jaime was ordered by his father to take one of the small tractors and plow the pumpkin vines under. The machine turned up the butterfly knife in the southeast corner of the field. It was an elegant little knife with a double handle which opened like a pair of wings and folded back to reveal the blade in the middle. One of Jaime's friends owned a butterfly knife. If you got the hang of it and practiced a lot in your spare time, the blade could be brought into striking position almost as fast as a switchblade, which was illegal.

Jaime was delighted with his find until he noticed the brownish crust around the hinges. He put the knife carefully down on the ground, wiped his hands on his jeans and went to tell his father.

SOUTH OF BOCA DE RIO the road met the main highway that connected San Diego and Tijuana. The two cities, so dissimilar in sight and sound and atmosphere, were bound together by geography and economics, like stepsisters with completely different backgrounds forced to live together under the same roof.

Within a matter of minutes Estivar and the station wagon were lost in the heavy flow of traffic. Leo Bishop drove in the slow lane, both hands so tight on the steering wheel that his knuckle bones seemed ready to force their way out of his skin. He was a tall thin man in his early forties. There was about him an air of defeat and bewilderment, as though all the rules he'd learned in life were, one by one, being reversed.

If Dulzura's youth was camouflaged by fat, Leo's age was exaggerated by years of sun and wind. His red hair was bleached to the color of sand, his face was scarred over his cheekbones and across the bridge of his nose by repeated burns. He had light green eyes which he protected from the sun by squinting, so that when he moved into the shade and his facial muscles relaxed, fine white lines appeared below and at the corners of his eyes where the ultraviolet rays hadn't reached. These lines gave him a curiously intense expression, which made some of the Mexicans whisper about *mal ojo,* evil eye, and *azar,* bad luck.

After his wife drowned in the river the whispers increased, he had trouble with his crews, equipment broke down, frost killed the grapefruit and damaged the date palms . . . *mal ojo . . . demonios del muerte.* He suspected Estivar of encouraging the rumors, but he never mentioned his suspicions to Devon. She would have trouble believing that evil eyes and demons were still part of Estivar's world.

"Devon."

"Yes?"

"It will soon be over."

She stirred, unbelieving. "What time is it?"

"Ten after nine."

"Mr. Ford said nothing would be settled today. Even if he manages to question all the witnesses, there'll still be a delay while the judge goes over the evidence. He may not announce his decision for a week, it depends on how much other work he has."

"At least your part will be over."

She wasn't sure what her part was going to be. The lawyer had instructed her not only to answer questions but to volunteer information whenever she felt like it, small personal things, homely things, that would help to show Robert as he really was. *"We want to make him come alive,"* Ford said. He did not apologize for the ill-chosen phrase; he seemed to be testing her composure to see if it would hold up in court.

The road had turned west toward San Diego Bay. Sail-

boats moved gently in the water like large white butterflies that had dipped down to drink. At the edge of the bay
a thin strand of beach, wet from the ebbing tide and sil-
vered by the sun, held back the open sea.

"You'd better let me off half a block or so from the
courthouse," Devon said. "Mrs. Osborne thinks we
shouldn't be seen together."

"Why?"

"People might talk."

"Would that matter?"

"It would to her."

They drove for a while without speaking. In the bay the
sailboats gave way to navy vessels, the white butterflies to
gray steel waterbugs with ferocious-looking antennae and
weird superstructures.

"After this is over," Leo said, "you won't have to be
quite so concerned about Agnes Osborne's opinions. She'll
be your ex-mother-in-law. Tomorrow, the day after, next
week, you'll be a free agent."

She repeated the phrase to herself, liking the sound of
it. Widow was a word of loss and sorrow. Free agent suggested the future. "And what do free agents do, Leo?"

"They make choices."

For Devon it had been a year without choices, a year
when all decisions were made by other people. She had
paid the bills Estivar told her to, signed the papers the
lawyer, Ford, put in front of her, answered the questions
asked by Valenzuela, the policeman, eaten what Dulzura
cooked, worn what Agnes Osborne suggested.

Soon the year would be officially over and the decisions
would be hers. There would be no more brown sharkskin
suits, no more *chorizo* and scrambled eggs hidden by chili
powder; Valenzuela wasn't even on the police force any
longer; after the conclusion of probate there would be no
reason to see Ford; she might sell the ranch, and then
Estivar, too, would become part of the past.

YSOBEL LEANED FORWARD to stare at the speedometer. "So we are in a race." Her voice was heavy with irony. "It is news to me that they hold races on the highway."

"The speed limit is sixty-five," Estivar said. "I have to keep up with the traffic."

"You'd think we were going to something nice like a fiesta the way you're in such a hurry to arrive. Mr. Bishop has more sense. He is miles behind us, and why not? He knows there's no prize waiting at the other end."

Estivar, who'd been in a sour mood all morning, suddenly let out a harsh, brief laugh. "You could be wrong about that."

"Hush. Someone might hear you and start putting two and two together."

She was not worried about Jaime, who seemed most of the time to be stone-deaf, or about Lum Wing, whose only Spanish, as far as she knew, consisted of some dirty words and a few seldom-used amenities like *buenos días.*

"You should be careful to guard your tongue when Dulzura is listening," Ysobel added. "She is a born gossip."

Dulzura opened her mouth in exaggerated amazement. It was not true she was a gossip, born or otherwise. She told nobody nothing, mainly because in such a godforsaken place there was nobody to tell except the people who already knew. She wondered what prize could be waiting for Mr. Bishop and how much it was worth and whether she should ask young Mrs. Osborne about it.

"The little Señora," Ysobel said more softly. "Is that what you mean by prize?"

"What else?"

"She would never marry him. He is too old."

"There isn't exactly a line-up at her door."

"Not yet. She is still by law a married woman and

cultivated people are very particular about such things. Just wait, after today there will be men enough, young men, too. But she'll have none of them. She'll sell the ranch and go back to the city."

"How do you know?"

"I dreamt it last night. In color. When I went to the fortune teller in Boca de Rio, she said to pay strict attention to all dreams in color because good or bad they would come true . . . Have you been dreaming in color, Estivar?"

"No."

"Oh well, it's no matter. This is how it will be: the little Señora will sell the ranch and return to her own part of the country."

"What about me?"

"The new owner will naturally be delighted to get a foreman with nearly twenty-five years of experience."

"Was that in the dream too, about the new owner?"

"No. But maybe I didn't watch closely enough. Tonight I will keep a sharp lookout for him standing in some corner."

"If he looks like Bishop," Estivar said grimly, "wake up fast."

"Bishop has no money to buy the ranch."

"He can marry it."

"No, no, no. The Señora is sick of the place. She will go back to the city, like in my dream. I saw her walking between tall gray buildings, wearing a purple dress and flowers in her hair."

Estivar's bad mood was aggravated by the exchange with his wife. The next time Lum Wing burped, Estivar shouted at him to stop making those damned noises or get out and walk.

Lum Wing would have preferred to get out and walk, but the car didn't stop to allow him to leave, and besides, there was that ominous piece of paper in his shirt pocket, *you better show up, by God, or else* . . . The old man was well aware that he had no control over his own fate. When other people were around, they decided what he should do. It was only when he was by himself that he had choices: solitaire or chess, lime in his gin or lemon, or no gin at all but a dozen or so jimsen seeds. To ensure his privacy, and his times of choice, he had fixed up a corner of the building which was used as a mess hall when the workers were in residence. Between the stove and the cupboard he'd hung a double flannelette sheet borrowed from one of the bunks. After his day's work was done he retired to his corner to play chess with imaginary partners who were very shrewd and merciless though not quite as shrewd and merciless as Lum Wing himself.

Half of the stove used butane as fuel, the other half used wood or coal. Even on warm nights Lum Wing kept a small fire going with bits of old lumber, or limbs pruned from the trees or blown off in windstorms. He liked the busy but impersonal noise of the burning wood. It helped cover what came out of the darkness on the other side of his flannelette wall—whispers, grunts, snatches of conversation, laughter.

Lum Wing tried to ignore these common sounds of common people and to keep his mind fixed on the ivory silence of kings and queens and knights. But there were times when in spite of himself he recognized a voice in the dark, and when this happened he made tiny plugs out of pieces of paper and pushed them as far into his ears as he could. He knew curiosity killed more men than cats.

He swallowed and regurgitated another mouthful of air.

". . . probably his liver," Ysobel said. "I have been told there are many contagious diseases of the liver." She took a handkerchief out of her purse and held it tight against her nose and mouth. Her sharp voice was muffled: "Jaime! Do you hear me, Jaime? Answer your mother."

"Answer your mother, Jaime," Dulzura said obligingly. "Hey, wake up."

Jaime's eyelids twitched slightly. "I'm awake."

"Well, answer your mother."

"So I'm answering. What's she want?"

"I don't know."

"Ask her."

Dulzura leaned over the front seat. "He wants to know what do you want?"

"Tell him not to let that Chinaman breathe in his face."

"She says don't let the Chinaman breathe in your face."

"He's not breathing in my face."

"Well, if he tries, don't let him."

Jaime closed his eyes again. The old lady was getting kookier every day. Personally, he hoped he'd be lucky like Mr. Osborne and die before he got senile.

ON THE COURTHOUSE STEPS pigeons preened in the sun and walked up and down, looking important like uniformed guards. Beside one of the colonnades Devon saw her lawyer, Franklin Ford, surrounded by half a dozen men. He caught her eye, gave her a quick warning glance and turned away again. As she went past she heard him speaking in his soft slow voice, enunciating each syllable very distinctly as though he were addressing a group of foreigners or idiots:

". . . bear in mind that this is a non-adversary proceeding. It is not being opposed by an insurance company, for instance, with a large policy to pay out on Robert Osborne's life, or by a relative who's not satisfied with the disposition of Mr. Osborne's estate. The amount of Mr. Osborne's insurance is negligible, consisting of a small policy taken out by his parents when he was a child. The terms of his will are clearly stated and have not been challenged; and of his survivors, his wife petitioned the court for this hearing and his mother concurred. So our purpose in today's hearing is to establish the fact of Robert Osborne's death and to prove as conclusively as possible how and why and when and where it occurred. Nobody has been accused, nobody is on trial."

As Devon went into the building she wondered which came closer to the truth, Ford's "Nobody is on trial," or Agnes Osborne's "Of course we are on trial, all of us."

The door of courtroom number five was open and the spectators' benches were nearly full. On the right side near the windows Agnes Osborne sat by herself. She wore a blue hat that perched like a jay on her careful blond curls, and a ribbon knit dress the same dark gray as her eyes. If she felt that she was on trial, she gave no sign of it. Her face was expressionless except for one corner of her mouth fixed in a half-smile, as though she was mildly, even a little contemptuously, amused by the situation and the company she found herself in. It was her public face. Her private one was uncertain, disordered, often blotched with tears and mottled with rage.

She watched Devon walk toward her down the aisle, thinking how incongruous she looked in this place of violence and death. Devon should still be wandering around the halls of some college with other nice mousy girls and earnest pimply boys. *I must be kinder to her, I must try harder to like her. It's my fault she's here.*

Mrs. Osborne had thought that if she sent Robert away from the ranch for a couple of months, the scandal about Ruth Bishop's death would blow over. It was a double error. His absence merely intensified the gossip, and when he returned he brought Devon with him as his wife. Agnes was shocked and hurt. She wanted her son to get married eventually, of course, but not at twenty-three, not to this odd little creature from another part of the world. *"Robert, why? Why did you do it?" "Why not? The girl loves me, she thinks I'm great. How about that!"*

25 /

Devon leaned over and the two women touched cheeks briefly. There was an air of finality about the cool embrace, as if both of them knew it would be one of the last.

AT THE BACK OF THE COURTROOM, sitting between his father and Dulzura, Jaime was like a patient coming out of an anesthetic and discovering that his moving parts could still move. He did a couple of secret isometric exercises, cleared his throat, hummed a few bars of a TV commercial —"Shut up," Estivar said—stuck another piece of gum in his mouth, pulled up his socks, cracked his knuckles— "Stop that!"—scratched his ear, rubbed one side of his jaw, pushed the greasy stump of a comb through his hair—"For God's sake, sit still, will you?"

Jaime crossed his arms over his chest and sat still except for the swinging of a foot against the bench in front and the practically inaudible grinding of his teeth. The scene was different from what he'd expected. He'd thought there would be a lot of fuzz hanging around. But in the whole courtroom only one cop was in sight, an old guy of thirty-five having a drink at the water cooler.

The judge's bench and the jury box were both empty. Between them a large drawing had been set up on an easel. Even by narrowing his eyes to slits and using all his powers of concentration, Jaime couldn't make out the contents of the drawing. Maybe it was left over from yesterday or last week and had nothing to do with Mr. Osborne. In spite of the cool act Jaime put on for his friends and the somnolent pose he assumed within the family circle, he still had the lively curiosity of a child.

He whispered to Dulzura, "Hey, move over so I can get out."

"Where you going?"

"Out, is all."

"You can get past."

"I can't. You're too fat."

"You're one fresh little big-mouth kid," Dulzura said and heaved herself up and into the aisle.

Casually, hands in pockets, Jaime walked to the front of the courtroom and sat down in the first row of benches. The cop had turned away from the water cooler and was watching him as though he suspected Jaime might pull a caper. Jaime tried to look like the kind of guy who could pull a caper if he wanted to but didn't feel like it at the moment.

The drawing on the easel was a map. What had appeared from the back of the room to be a road was the riverbed which marked the east and southeast boundaries of the ranch. The little triangles were trees, indicating the lemon orchard on the west, on the northeast the avocado grove, and on the north the rows of date palms with grapefruit growing in the shade between. The circle showed the location of the reservoir; and the rectangles, each of them lettered, were buildings: the ranch house itself, the mess hall, the bunkhouse and storage sheds, the garage for all the mechanized equipment and, on the other side of the garage, the house where Jaime lived with his family.

"Are you looking for something, fellow?" the cop said.

"No. I mean, no, sir. I was just studying the map. It shows where I live. The square marked C, that's my house."

"No kidding."

"I'm a witness in the case."

"Is that a fact."

"I was driving the tractor when suddenly I looked down on the ground and there was this knife lying there."

"Well, well, well. You'd better go back to your seat. The judge is coming in and he likes things tidy."

"Don't you want to know what kind of knife it was?"

"I can wait. I have to sit through the whole thing anyway, I'm the bailiff."

The clerk of the court, a young man wearing horn-rimmed glasses and a blue serge suit, got up and made the first of his four daily announcements: "Superior Court of the State of California in and for the County of San Diego is now in session, Judge Porter Gallagher presiding. Please be seated."

The clerk took his place at the table he shared with the bailiff. The hearing of probate petitions was usually the dullest of all judicial procedures, but this one promised to be different. Before putting it aside to file, he read part of the petition again.

In the Matter of the Estate of Robert Kirkpatrick Osborne, Deceased, the petition of Devon Suellen Osborne respectfully shows:

That she is the surviving wife of Robert Osborne.

That Petitioner is informed and believes and upon such information and belief alleges that Robert Osborne is dead. The precise time of his death is not known, but Petitioner believes and therefore alleges that Robert Osborne died on the thirteenth day of October, 1967. The facts upon which the death of Robert Osborne is presumed are as follows:

The Petitioner and her husband, Robert Osborne, lived together as husband and wife for approximately half a year. On the night of October 13, Robert Osborne, after dining with his wife, left the ranch house to look for his dog, which had wandered off in the course of the evening. When Robert Osborne failed to return by half past nine, Mrs. Robert Osborne roused the foreman of the ranch and a search was organized. It was the first of many searches covering a period of many months and an area of hundreds of square miles.

Evidence has been collected which proves beyond a reasonable doubt that between 8:30 and 9:30 o'clock on the night of October 13, 1967, Robert Osborne met his death at the hands of two or more persons . . .

CHAPTER
THREE

JUDGE GALLAGHER tugged impatiently at the collar of his black judicial robe. Even after fifteen years on the bench he still dreaded this moment when he walked into the courtroom and people stared up at him as if they expected the robe to endow him with magic qualities like Batman's cape. Occasionally, when he caught a particularly anxious eye, he wanted to take time out to explain that the robe was merely a piece of cloth covering a business suit, a drip-dry shirt and an ordinary man who couldn't perform miracles no matter how badly they were needed.

Gallagher looked around the room, noting with surprise that the only empty seats were those in the jury box. To his knowledge there'd been no publicity about the hearing except the legal notices in the newspapers. Perhaps the legal notices had a larger public than he imagined. More likely, though, some of the people were drop-ins who had no real interest in the case: the lady shopper resting her feet between sales; the young marine who seemed to be suffering from a hangover; a small group of high school students with notebooks and clipboards; a teen-aged girl, thin as a reed, carrying a sleeping baby and wearing a blond wig and sunglasses as big as saucers.

Some of the spectators were courtroom regulars who came for the excitement and because they had nowhere else to go. A middle-aged German woman knitted with speed and equanimity through embezzlement trials, divorces, armed robberies and rapes. A pair of elderly pensioners, one man on crutches, the other carrying a white cane, appeared even in the worst weather to sit through the dullest cases. They carried sandwiches in their pockets and at noon they would eat outside on the steps, feeding the crusts to the pigeons. To Gallagher, looking down on them from the windows of his chambers, it seemed a very good way to spend the noon hour.

Even without years of practice it would have been easy for Gallagher to pick out the people closely connected with the case: Osborne's wife and mother pretending to be cool in the heat of the morning; some leather-faced ranchers looking out of place and uneasy in their city clothes; the ex-policeman, Valenzuela, almost unrecognizable in a natty striped suit and orange tie; and sitting at the counsels' table, Mrs. Osborne's lawyer, Ford, a soft-spoken, gentle-mannered man with a ferocious temper that had cost him hundreds of dollars in contempt fines.

"Are you ready, Mr. Ford?"

"Yes, your Honor."

"Then go ahead."

"This is a proceeding to establish the death of Robert Kirkpatrick Osborne. In support of the allegations contained in the petition of Devon Suellen Osborne, I intend to submit a considerable amount of evidence. I beg the indulgence of the court in the manner of submitting this evidence.

"Your Honor, the body of Robert Osborne has not been found. Under California law, death is a rebuttable presumption after an absence of seven years. The presumption of death before this seven-year period has passed requires circumstantial evidence to show first, the fact of death, i.e., there must be enough evidence from which a reasonable conclusion can be reached that death has occurred; and second, that absence from any cause other than death is inconsistent with the nature of the person absent.

"The following quote is from the People versus L. Ewing Scott: Any evidence, facts or circumstances concerning the alleged deceased, relating to the character, long absence without communicating with friends or relatives, habits, condition, affections, attachments, prosperity and objects in life which usually control the conduct of a person and are the motive of such person's actions, and the absence of any evidence to show the motive or cause for the abandonment of home, family or friends or wealth by the alleged deceased, are competent evidence from which may be inferred the death of one absent or unheard from, whatever has been the duration or shortness of such absence. Unquote.

"We intend to show, your Honor, that Robert Osborne was a young man of twenty-four, mentally and physically well-endowed, happily married and the owner of a prospering ranch; that his relationship with his family, friends and neighbors was pleasant, that he was enjoying life and looking forward to the future.

33 /

"If we could follow any man around on any particular day of his life, we would find out a great deal about him, his character, the state of his health, his mind, his finances, his interests, hobbies, plans, ambitions. I can think of no better way of presenting a true picture of Robert Osborne than to reconstruct, as completely as I am able, his final day. Bear with me, your Honor, if I elicit from witnesses details that are seemingly irrelevant, and opinions, suppositions and conclusions that would not be admissible evidence in an adversary proceeding.

"The final day was October 13, 1967. It started on the Yerba Buena ranch, where Robert Osborne was born and where he lived most of his life. The weather was very warm, as it had been since early spring, and the river was dry. A late crop of tomatoes was being harvested and crated for shipping, and the picking of dates was scheduled to begin. The ranch was a busy place and Robert Osborne a busy young man.

"On October 13 he awoke before dawn as usual and began his preparations for the day. While he was in the shower his wife, Devon, also awoke but she didn't get up. She was in the early stage of a difficult pregnancy and under doctor's orders to stay as quiet as possible ... I would like to call as my first witness, Devon Suellen Osborne."

The courtroom stirred, rustled, whispered, shifted its weight. Then everything was suddenly quiet again as Devon walked toward the stand. *"Do you swear . . . ?"* She swore, her raised right hand steady, her voice flat. Ford could scarcely remember the wild weeping girl of a year ago.

"Would you state your name for the record, please?"

"Devon Suellen Osborne."

"And where do you live?"

"Rancho Yerba Buena, Rural Route number two."

"Displayed on the easel is a map. Have you seen it before?"

"Yes, in your office."

"And you had a chance to study it?"

"Yes."

"Is it a true representation of a portion of the property known as Rancho Yerba Buena?"

"To my knowledge it is."

"Do you own any portion of Rancho Yerba Buena, Mrs. Osborne?"

"No. The deed has been in my husband's name since he was twenty-one."

"During the early part of Mr. Osborne's absence, how was the ranch business carried on?"

"It wasn't. Bills piled up, checks came in which couldn't be cashed, purchases were at a standstill. That's when I went to you for help."

Ford turned to Judge Gallagher. "Your Honor, I advised Mrs. Osborne to wait until ninety days had elapsed from the time her husband had last been seen and then appeal to the court to appoint her as trustee of the missing man's estate. The appointment was granted, Mrs. Osborne was bonded, as required, and through my office made periodic accountings to the court of receipts and disbursements and the like."

"And that is your present position, Mrs. Osborne," Gallagher said, "trustee of the estate?"

"Yes, your Honor."

"Continue, Mr. Ford."

Ford went over to the map and pointed to the small rectangle bearing the letter O. "Is this the ranch house, Mrs. Osborne?"

"Yes."

"And it was here that you saw your husband before sunrise on October 13 last year?"

"Yes."

"Did any conversation take place at that time?"

"Nothing important."

"In the reconstruction of a man's final day it is difficult to say what's important and what isn't. Tell us the things you remember, Mrs. Osborne."

"It was still dark. I woke up when Robert came out of the shower and turned on the bureau lamp. He asked me how I felt and I said fine. While he was getting dressed we talked about various matters."

"Was there anything unusual about the way he dressed that morning?"

"He put on slacks and a sports jacket instead of his working clothes because he was driving into the city."

"This city, San Diego?"

"Yes."

"Would you describe the slacks and jacket, Mrs. Osborne?"

"The slacks were lightweight gray gabardine and the jacket was gray and black dacron in a small plaid pattern."

"Why was he driving into San Diego?"

"A number of reasons. In the morning he had a dental appointment, and after that he was going to drop in and see his mother and then pick up a tennis racket he'd ordered, one of the new kind made of steel. I reminded him too that it was Dulzura's birthday—she is our cook—and that he should buy her a present."

"Did he, in fact, do all of these things?"

"Except the present, he forgot that."

"Wasn't there a luncheon meeting at noon which he was expected to attend?"

"Yes."

"Do you know what the meeting was about?"

"It concerned problems of migrant labor in California agriculture."

"Did he go to the meeting?"

"Yes. Robert had the idea that the problem must be solved at the source, the crops themselves. If crops could be regulated chemically, such as by hormones, perhaps harvesting could become a twelve-month-a-year business which would give steady employment to agricultural workers and do away entirely with migrant labor."

"Now, Mrs. Osborne, that morning after your husband finished dressing, what did he do?"

"He kissed me goodbye and told me he'd be home for dinner about seven-thirty. He also asked me to keep a sharp lookout for his spaniel, Maxie, who'd taken off the night before. I thought Maxie had caught the scent of a bitch in heat and gone to find her, but Robert suspected something more sinister might be involved."

"Such as?"

"He didn't say. But Maxie was never allowed near the bunkhouse or the mess hall, and at night he was kept inside the house."

"Was this for the dog's protection or yours?"

"Both. At certain times of the year there were quite a few strangers around the ranch. Maxie was our watchdog and we were—well, I guess you could call us his watchpeople."

At the unusual word a little hum of laughter vibrated through the courtroom and bounced gently off the walls.

"The dog, then," Ford continued, "was not friendly toward any of the workers on the ranch?"

"No."

"In the event of an attack on your husband, do you think the dog would have gone to his defense?"

"I know he would."

Ford sat down at the counsels' table and spread his hands in front of him, palms up, as if he intended to read in their lines the past as well as the future. "When and where were you and Robert Osborne married?"

"April 24, 1967, in Manhattan."

"How old was Mr. Osborne at that time?"

"Twenty-three."

"Had you known him long?"

"Two weeks."

"Since you were willing to marry him after so brief an acquaintance, I must assume he made a considerable impression on you."

"Yes."

A considerable impression.

They had met at a Saturday afternoon concert at the Philharmonic. Devon arrived during the opening number and slipped quietly and apologetically into her seat. As her eyes gradually adjusted to the darkness she became aware that the seat on her left was occupied by a large young man with fair hair and horn-rimmed glasses. Every minute or two he turned to stare at her and at intermission he followed her into the lobby. She wasn't used to such uninvited attention and it made her a little uneasy and more than a little curious. The young man gave the impression of having walked into the concert hall either by mistake or because someone had given him a ticket and he didn't want to waste it.

She was the first to speak. "Why are you staring at me?"

"Was I staring?"

"You still are."

"Sorry." His smile was shy, almost melancholy. "I guess I can't help it. You remind me of someone back home."

"Someone nice, I hope."

"She used to be."

"Isn't she nice any more?"

"No."

"Why not?"

"She's dead." After a moment's hesitation he added, "A lot of people think I killed her. I didn't, but when people want to believe something, it's hard to stop them."

Now it was Devon who stared, and a pulse began to beat rapidly in the back of her head like a warning signal. "You shouldn't go around saying things like that to strangers."

"I never did before. I wish you'd—"

But she had already started to walk away.

"Please wait," he said. "Did I frighten you? I'm sorry. It was a dumb thing to do. It's just that I haven't talked to anyone since I came to town and you looked nice and gentle like Ruth."

Her name was Ruth, Devon thought. *She looked nice and gentle and a lot of people think this young man killed her and maybe he did.*

"I'm sorry I frightened you," he said. "Wait just a minute, will you?"

She turned to face him. "Appearances are deceiving. I'm not very nice and not at all gentle, so you'd better forget whatever you had in mind."

"But—"

"And I suggest that for the balance of the concert you go and sit somewhere else."

"All right."

For the next hour the seat beside her remained empty. She wanted to look around to see if he was sitting anywhere nearby but she forced herself to keep her eyes on the stage and to concentrate on the music, applauding when other people applauded.

After the concert he was waiting for her in the lobby. "Miss? Would you let me talk to you for a minute? I've been thinking over what a stupid thing I did. It's no wonder you were scared."

"I wasn't scared. I was annoyed."

"I'm sorry. My only excuse is that I felt I should be honest with you right from the start."

"There hasn't been a start," she said. "Nothing has started. Now if you'll—"

"My name is Robert Osborne, Robert Kirkpatrick Osborne. What's yours?"

"Devon Suellen Smith."

"I like that. It's pretty."

While she explained that her parents wanted something different to make up for the "Smith," she became aware that she'd been wrong and the young man right: there was a start.

It continued through coffee and éclairs at Schrafft's, and the next morning they met for a walk in Central Park. It was the first warm Sunday of the year. There must have been people everywhere in the park, but the only one Devon could remember seeing was Robert as he strode across the grass toward her, his pockets bulging with peanuts he'd bought to feed the squirrels. He told her about his ranch in California, which was really a farm, and about the squirrels on it that lived in holes in the ground instead of trees. He talked about Maxie, the spaniel; about his father, who had died years ago in a fall off a tractor; about the land, which was irrigated desert, and the crazy river that was either flooding or bone-dry. By the end of the day Devon knew that her life had changed abruptly and would never be the same again.

". . . please respond to the question, Mrs. Osborne?"

"I'm sorry, I didn't hear it."

"Was your husband a big man?"

"Six feet one and about a hundred and seventy pounds."

"He was in good health?"

"Yes."

"Active and strong?"

"Yes."

"Did he have any physical disabilities? For instance, did he wear glasses?"

"Yes."

"What kind?"

"To correct his short-sightedness—I think myopia is the right word."

"Did he have more than one pair?"

"Yes. Besides his ordinary horn-rimmed glasses he had

prescription sunglasses which he used especially while driving. During the early part of the summer he'd been fitted with contact lenses, and he wore them for tennis and swimming and other times when his ordinary glasses would have been a nuisance."

"These contact lenses were prescribed and fitted by an ophthalmologist?"

"Yes."

"Do you happen to recall his name?"

"Dr. Jarrett."

"Where is his office?"

"Here in San Diego."

Ford consulted some notes on the table in front of him. "Now, Mrs. Osborne, you stated that one of your husband's reasons for driving to the city was to pick up a new tennis racket he'd ordered. Did he actually try the racket out during the afternoon?"

"Yes. He played several sets on one of the courts in Balboa Park."

"Did he wear his contact lenses?"

"Yes."

"Are you certain of this?"

"I'm certain that he was wearing them when he got home."

"Did he continue to wear them through dinner?"

"Yes."

"And after dinner when he went out looking for the dog, Maxie, was he still wearing the contact lenses?"

"Yes."

"Who has these lenses at the present time, Mrs. Osborne?"

"The police."

"What about his prescription sunglasses—where are they now?"

"In the glove compartment of his car."

"Where he left them?"

"Yes."

"What about his ordinary horn-rimmed glasses? Where are they now?"

"I don't know."

"You mean they were lost or misplaced?"

"Neither."

"When was the last time you saw them, Mrs. Osborne?"

"Three weeks ago. If you want the exact time it was the day you phoned to tell me this hearing had been scheduled. My husband's glasses were among other things of his which I packed in cartons. I intended to store the cartons in the attic. Then I realized that this would be merely postponing the inevitable, so I decided to give the stuff to the Salvation Army in the hope that some use could be made of it. I know Robert would have approved."

"Did you deliver it to the Salvation Army yourself?"

"No. Mrs. Osborne, Robert's mother, offered to do it."

"When you were packing those cartons, were you pretty sure what the outcome of today's hearing would be?"

"I was sure my husband was dead. I'd been sure for a long time."

"Why?"

"Nothing would keep Robert from getting in touch with me if he were alive."

"You were happily married?"

"Yes."

"And expecting a child?"

"Yes."

"Did you carry the child to term, Mrs. Osborne?"

"No."

SHE REMEMBERED THE TRIP to the hospital in the back of Estivar's station wagon, with Dulzura beside her, strangely silent and dignified, and a police car clearing the way, its siren screaming. It took a long time to come home from the hospital. Autumn was nearly over, the migrants were gone, the crops harvested.

The return trip was quieter. There was no police escort. She rode in a taxicab instead of the station wagon, with Agnes Osborne beside her instead of Dulzura. Mrs. Osborne talked to her in a flat, low-pitched voice which gave no indication that the loss of the child was a more severe blow to her than it was to Devon. For Devon there would be other chances, for Mrs. Osborne it was the end of the line. She told Devon what to do, sounding as though she were reading off a list she'd written down in a corner of her mind: get lots of sleep and fresh air, avoid worry, be brave, exercise, replace Dulzura with a more responsible person, take up a hobby, eat plenty of protein . . .

". . . attention to me, Devon?"

"Yes."

"We'd probably be wise to ignore Christmas this year, it's such an emotional occasion anyway. Perhaps you'd enjoy going off on a little holiday by yourself. Don't you have an aunt in Buffalo?"

"Please stop bothering about me."

"I hate the thought of you staying alone at the ranch. It's not safe. Dulzura is unreliable, you should be aware of that by now."

"I know she drinks a little bit now and then."

"She drinks a whole lot and whenever she can get her hands on the stuff. As for Estivar, how can we really tell whose side he'd be on in an emergency? He's learned English and the ranching business and a few manners in the last twenty-five years, but he's just as Mexican now as when he crossed the border— What happened to your aunt in Buffalo?"

"She died."

"Everyone's dying. Oh God, I can't stand it. Everyone's dying . . ."

FORD GOT UP, walked slowly around the end of the counsels' table and stood leaning against the railing of the empty jury box. The move was deliberate, to give Devon a chance to compose herself.

"Mrs. Osborne, you stated previously that before your husband left the house on the morning of October 13 he told you he'd be back for dinner at seven-thirty. Did he come back by seven-thirty?"

"Yes."

"And you had dinner together."

"Yes."

"Was it a pleasant meal?"

"Yes."

"And when it was over, Mr. Osborne went outside to try and find the dog, Maxie."

"Yes."

"What time was that?"

"Eight-thirty, approximately."

"After he left the house, what did you do?"

"A new record album had arrived in the mail that day and I played it."

"How big an album?"

"Three records, six sides."

"What kind of music was it?"

"Symphonic."

"In most symphonies there are soft passages which require the volume to be turned up quite high if they are to be heard properly. Was the volume turned up high, Mrs. Osborne?"

"Yes."

"This would make the louder passages very loud, would it not?"

"Yes."

"Where in the ranch house was the stereo equipment installed?"

"The main living room."

"And that's where you sat and listened to the album?"

"Yes, but I didn't just sit. I walked around, did some dusting and straightening up, glanced at the evening paper."

"Were the windows closed or open?"

"Closed. It was a hot night and the house stayed cooler when it was shut up."

"What about the drapes?"

"I opened them after the sun went down."

"What direction do the windows in the living room face?"

"East and south."

"What do you see from the windows facing east?"

"In the daytime I can see the riverbed and, on the other side of it, the ranch belonging to Leo Bishop."

"And at night?"

"Nothing."

"Is there a view from the windows facing south?"

"You can see Tijuana in the distance both night and day."

"What about the blacktop road leading into the ranch, is this visible from the main living room?"

"No. It's west of the ranch house. You can see it from the study and the kitchen and a couple of the bedrooms upstairs."

"But not from the living room where you were sitting listening to music."

"Not from there, no."

Ford went back to the counsels' table and sat down. "As time passed and your husband remained absent, did you begin to worry, Mrs. Osborne?"

"I tried to tell myself there was nothing to worry about,

that Robert had been born on the ranch and knew every inch of it. But around nine forty-five I decided to check the garage to see if maybe Robert had taken the car to search for Maxie instead of going on foot as he usually did. I turned on the outside floodlights from the kitchen. Dulzura was in her room adjoining the kitchen, I could hear the radio playing."

"Did you find the garage door unlocked?"

"Yes."

"Was Mr. Osborne's car in the garage?"

"Yes."

"What did you do then, Mrs. Osborne?"

"I went back in the house and telephoned Mr. Estivar."

"The foreman?"

"Yes. His cottage is on the other side of the reservoir."

"Did he answer immediately?"

"No. He goes to bed around nine and it was almost ten by this time. But I let the phone keep ringing until he woke up and answered. I told him Robert was missing, and he said I was to stay in the house with all the doors and windows locked while he and Cruz made a search with the jeep."

"Cruz?"

"Estivar's oldest son. He had a jeep with a searchlight on it."

"Did you do as Mr. Estivar suggested?"

"Yes. I waited in the kitchen by the window. I could see the lights of the jeep as it went up and down the little dirt roads that crisscross the ranch."

"Did you notice any other signs of activity, any vehicles in motion, any people, any lights?"

"No."

"Is it possible to see the mess hall and the bunkhouse from any of the windows of the ranch house?"

"No. A row of tamarisk trees shields the main house from the men's quarters."

"How long did you wait in the kitchen, Mrs. Osborne?"

"Until a quarter to eleven, about forty-five minutes."

"Then what happened?"

"Mr. Estivar came to the door."

"Was he alone?"

"Yes."

"What did he say to you?"

"He said we'd better notify the police."

"And did you?"

"Mr. Estivar called the sheriff's office in Boca de Rio."

"The sheriff's men arrived when, Mrs. Osborne?"

"Shortly after eleven o'clock. The man in charge was Mr. Valenzuela. The other man was younger, I don't recall his name, but he was the one who found all the—the blood in the mess hall."

"Were you informed of his discovery?"

"Not directly. Mr. Valenzuela came back to the ranch house about eleven-thirty and asked if he could use the phone to call the sheriff's office in San Diego. I overheard him say that a great deal of blood had been found and it looked like the result of a homicide."

"What did you do then, Mrs. Osborne?"

"Dulzura was up by that time. She made a pot of coffee and I think I drank some. Pretty soon I heard a siren. I'd never heard a siren on the ranch before, it's always so quiet late at night. I looked out the kitchen window and saw several cars moving along the road and red lights flashing."

IN ADDITION TO THE SIREN there was the sound of Dulzura praying in Spanish, very loudly, as though she had a bad connection. Then suddenly the cuckoo clock above the stove began striking midnight, a mocking reminder that Robert had been gone for three and a half hours and it might be too late for prayers or policemen.

Devon went into the study, closing the door behind her to shut out some of the noise. For the first time she became physically aware of the child in her womb. It felt heavy and inert as a marble cherub.

She dialed the number of Agnes Osborne's house in San Diego. Mrs. Osborne answered on the third ring, sounding a little annoyed, as though she'd been watching a late show on TV and didn't like being interrupted by a wrong number.

"Mother?"

"Is that you, Devon? Why aren't you in bed at this hour? The doctor told you—"

"I think something's happened to Robert."

"—get plenty of sleep. What did you say?"

"The police are here now searching for him. He went out to look for Maxie and he hasn't come back and there's blood in the mess hall, a lot of blood."

There was a long silence, then Mrs. Osborne's voice again, stubbornly cheerful. "It's not the first time blood's been found in the mess hall. Why, I can remember a dozen brawls in there, three or four of them quite serious. The men frequently quarrel among themselves, and of course they all carry knives. Are you listening to me, Devon?"

"Yes."

"What probably happened is this: while Robert was out looking for the dog he heard a fight going on in the mess hall and went in to investigate. Perhaps one of the men was badly injured and Robert had to drive him into Boca de Rio to a doctor."

"No."

"What do you mean, *no?*"

"He didn't drive anywhere. His car's here."

There was another long pause. Then, "I'll come right out. For the baby's sake, don't get overexcited. I'm sure there's a perfectly logical explanation and Robert will be quite amused when he learns that the police were looking for him. Do you have any tranquilizers to take?"

"No."

"I'll bring some with me."

"I don't want any." There was no need to tranquilize the stone mother of a marble cherub . . .

". . . ANY MORE QUESTIONS at this time," Ford was saying. "You are excused for now, Mrs. Osborne."

He watched with interest as she stepped down from the witness stand and went back to her place in the spectators' benches. Long experience in probate work had taught Ford to be suspicious of meek little women. They had a tendency to inherit if not the earth, at least some large chunks of worldly goods.

"Call Mr. Secundo Estivar."

CHAPTER
FOUR

FORD SAID, "Please state your full name for the record."

"Secundo Alvino Juan Estivar."

"And your address?"

"Rancho Yerba Buena."

"That is the area depicted on the map to your left?"

"Yes, sir."

"You're employed there?"

"Yes."

"In what capacity?"

"Foreman."

"You're responsible for the operation of the ranch?"

"The court appointed young Mrs. Osborne boss during Mr. Osborne's absence. I take orders from her. If there are no such orders, I do the best I can without them." A suffusion of scarlet spread across Estivar's cheeks and into the whites of his eyes. "When the ranch makes money, I don't claim any credit; when there's a robbery and a murder, I'm not about to take the blame."

"No one is putting the blame on you."

"Not in words. But I can smell it a mile away, so I think I'd better clear something up right now. I hire people in good faith. If it turns out their names and addresses are phony and their papers forged, that's not my fault. I'm not a cop. How can I tell whether papers are forged or not?"

"Kindly simmer down, Mr. Estivar."

"I'm in the hot seat, it's not so easy to simmer down."

"Suppose you try," Ford said. "A couple of weeks ago, when you and I discussed your appearance here as a witness, I told you this proceeding is to establish the fact that a death has occurred, not to hold anyone responsible for the death."

"You told me that. But—"

"Then please bear it in mind, will you?"

"Yes."

"When did you first arrive at the Osborne ranch, Mr. Estivar?"

"In 1943."

"From where?"

"A little village near Empalme."

"And where is Empalme?"

"In Sonora, México."

"Were you carrying border-crossing papers?"

"No."

"Did you have any trouble finding employment without such papers?"

"No. There was a war on. Growers needed help, they

couldn't afford to bother about little things like immigration laws. Hundreds of Mexicans like me walked across that border every week and found jobs."

"A lot of them are still doing it, are they not?"

"Yes."

"In fact, there's a profitable underground business in Mexico which consists of supplying such men with forged papers and transportation."

"So I've heard."

"We'll go into this subject more thoroughly a little later in the hearing," Ford said. "Who hired you to work on the Osborne ranch in 1943?"

"Robert Osborne's father, John."

"Have you worked there steadily since then?"

"Yes, sir."

"So your relationship with Robert Osborne goes back a long time."

"To the day he was born."

"Was it a close relationship?"

"From the time he could walk he followed me around like a pup. I saw more of him than I did my own kids. He called me Tío—uncle."

"Did this relationship continue throughout his life?"

"No. The summer he was fifteen his father was killed in an accident, and things changed after that. For all of us, I guess, but especially for the boy. In the fall he was sent off to a prep school in Arizona. His mother thought he needed the influence of men—she meant white men." Estivar glanced briefly at Agnes Osborne as though he expected her to issue a public denial. But she had turned her head away and was looking out the window at a patch of sky. "He stayed at the school two years. When he returned he wasn't a kid any more tagging along behind me asking questions or coming over to my house for meals. He was the boss and I was the hired man. And that's the way it stayed until the day he died."

"Was there any ill-will between Mr. Osborne and yourself?"

"We disagreed once in a while, about business, nothing personal. We had nothing personal between us any more, just the ranch. We both wanted to operate the ranch as profitably as we could, which meant that sometimes I had to take orders I didn't like and Mr. Osborne had to accept advice he didn't want."

"Would you say there was mutual respect between you?"

"No, sir. Mutual interest. Mr. Osborne had no respect for me or any other members of my race. It was that school she sent—he was sent to. That's what changed him. It taught him prejudice. I was used to prejudice, I'd learned to live with it. But how could I explain to my sons that their friend Robbie didn't exist any more? I didn't know the reason. I thought many times of asking her—his mother—but I never did. After he died it bothered me that I didn't try harder to find out why he'd changed, maybe talked it over with him like in the old days. Deep down I kind of expected that eventually he'd tell me all about it on his own and I shouldn't try to hurry it because there was lots of time. But there wasn't."

Estivar stopped to wipe the beads of sweat off his forehead. A hush had fallen over the courtroom, as if each person in it were straining to hear the sound of time running out, the slow drag of the minutes, the quick tick of years. Ford said, "On the morning of October 13, 1967, did you see Robert Osborne?"

"Yes, sir."

"What were the circumstances?"

"Very early, while it was still dark, I heard him whistling for his dog, Maxie. About half an hour later my wife and I were eating our breakfast when Mr. Osborne came to the back door and asked me to step outside. He sounded upset and mad, so I got out there fast as I could. The dog was lying on the ground with froth all around its mouth and its eyes kind of dazed-looking, like it might have been hit on the head or something."

"You stated that Mr. Osborne was 'upset and mad.'"

"Yes, sir. He said, 'Some filthy so-and-so around here poisoned my dog.' Only he didn't say 'so-and-so,' he used a very insulting term meaning the lowest kind of Mexican. For myself, I don't care about names. But my family heard it, my wife and my younger children who were still at the breakfast table. I ordered Mr. Osborne to go away and to stay away until he had his temper under control."

"Did he do so?"

"Yes, sir. He picked the dog up in his arms and left."

"Did you see Mr. Osborne again later?"

Estivar rubbed the back of his hand across his mouth. "No."

"Will you please speak louder?"

"That was the last time I saw him, heading for the ranch house with the dog in his arms. The last words we spoke to each other were in anger. It weighs heavy on me, that goodbye."

"I'm sure it does. Still, it was not your fault."

"Some of it was. I knew how much the little dog meant to him. It had been a present years ago from someone who —from a friend."

Ford began pacing up and down in front of the empty jury box, partly from habit, partly from impatience. "Now, Mr. Estivar, it is not my intention during this hearing to explore the complicated subject of migrant labor in California agriculture. We must, however, establish certain facts which affect the case, bearing in mind that you, as foreman, are caught in the middle of the problem. On the one hand you represent the growers whose business it is to market the crops for a profit. On the other hand you are aware that the present system—or lack of system—encourages the breaking of laws on the part of Mexican nationals, and the exploitation of these nationals on the part of the growers. Is that a fair statement of your situation, Mr. Estivar?"

"Fair enough, I guess."

"All right, we'll proceed. In the late summer and early fall of 1967, who was employed at the Osborne ranch besides yourself?"

"In August my three oldest sons were there, Cruz, Rufo and Felipe. My cousin, Dulzura Gonzales, acted as the Osbornes' housekeeper, and my youngest boy, Jaime, worked several hours a day. We employed half a dozen border-crossers, Mexican citizens with permits that allowed them to cross the border every day and work on ranches within commuting distance. We also had a part-time mechanic who came out from Boca de Rio to service the machinery."

"That was in August, you said."

"Yes, sir."

"Were you using any migrant labor at the time?"

"No. We couldn't get any. The grape strike was going on up in Delano and Mexican nationals were being used as strikebreakers. A lot of them were lured away from this area by the promise of higher wages in the vineyards up north; the rest were taken by the larger growers. The Osborne ranch is a comparatively small family operation."

"What happened in September with regard to this operation?"

"Plenty, all of it bad. My second son, Rufo, got married and went to live in Salinas so his wife could be near her family. My third son, Felipe, left to try and find employment in another line. I lost even Jaime, because school started and he could only help on Saturdays. The border-crossers had their minibus stolen off a street in Tijuana and couldn't come to work without transportation. By the end of the month only Cruz, my oldest son, was still with me working full-time. We were putting in sixteen-hour days until that old G.M. truck arrived with the men in it."

"You're referring to the men you subsequently hired to harvest tomatoes and dates."

" 'Subsequently' makes it sound like I sat around thinking about it first. I didn't. I hired them as soon as they could pile out of the truck. Then I phoned Lum Wing at his daughter's place in Boca de Rio and told him he had a job cooking for a new crew."

"How many men were in this crew, Mr. Estivar?"

"Ten."

"Were they strangers to you?"

"Yes."

"They were not, as far as you knew, wetbacks or *alambres.*"

"No. They were *viseros,* Mexican nationals registered as farm hands with visas that allowed them to work in this country. Anglos usually called them green-carders because the visas are in the form of green cards."

"Did the crew present their visas, or green cards, to you?"

"Yes."

"What did you do then?"

"I told the men they were hired and entered their names and addresses in my books. My son, Cruz, showed them where they were to eat and sleep and store their gear."

"Did they have much gear?"

"Migrants travel light," Estivar said. "They live light."

"Did you examine the visas carefully when they were presented to you?"

"I looked at them. Like I mentioned before, I'm not a cop, there's no way for me to tell by looking at a visa whether it's genuine or not. If I hadn't hired those men they'd have just gone over to Mr. Bishop's place across the river or to the Polks' ranch east of that. All the small growers were desperate for help because of the *huelga,* the grape strike, and because it was the height of the harvesting season."

"Did the crew have a leader?"

"I'm not sure you could call him a leader exactly, but the man who drove the truck did most of the talking."

"You said it was an old G.M. truck."

"Yes."

"How old?"

"Very. It was burning so much oil ·it looked like a smokestack."

"Who owned the truck?"

"I don't know."

"Didn't you check the vehicle registration?"

"No."

"Why not?"

"I never thought of it. Why should I? If you drove up to the ranch and asked for a job picking tomatoes, I wouldn't check your car registration."

Ford raised a quizzical eyebrow. "Would you give me a job, Mr. Estivar?"

"I might. But you wouldn't last." There was a burst of laughter from the spectators. Estivar did not join in. Color had spread across his face again except for a thin white line around his mouth. "You're too tall. Tall men have a rough time doing stoop labor."

"What day was it when the crew arrived at the ranch in the old G.M. truck?"

"September 28, a Thursday."

"So that by the time Robert Osborne disappeared, October 13, the men had been working at the ranch for two weeks."

"Yes, sir."

"Did you get to know any of them personally?"

"I don't run a social club."

"Still, it's possible that one or two of the men might

have told you about their wives and families back home, things like that."

"It may be possible but it didn't happen. The men were paid by the lug. They didn't want to talk any more than I wanted to listen."

"How often were they paid, Mr. Estivar?"

"Once a week, same as all the other crews."

"On what day?"

"Friday. Mr. Osborne wrote the checks on Thursday night and I handed them out in the mess hall while the men were having breakfast."

"What did they do after work on payday?"

"I don't know for sure."

"Well, what do crews usually do?"

"They go into Boca de Rio and cash their checks. The bank is closed on Saturday, so on Friday nights it stays open until six. The men settle accounts with each other and some of them buy money orders to send back home. They go to the laundromat, the grocery store, the movies, a bar. There's usually a crap game in somebody's back room or garage. A few get drunk and start fights, but they're generally pretty quiet about it because they don't want to attract the attention of the Border Patrol."

"What kind of fights?"

"With knives, mostly."

"Do they all carry knives?"

"Knives are often used in their work. They're tools, not just weapons."

"All right, Mr. Estivar, did the crew that was working for you on October 13, 1967, leave the ranch right after work?"

"Yes, sir."

"In the truck?"

"Yes."

"Did they return that night?"

"I was just going to bed when I heard the truck drive

in shortly after nine and park outside the bunkhouse."

"How do you know it was the old G.M.?"

"The brakes had a peculiar squeak. Besides, no other vehicle was likely to park in that particular spot."

"Nine o'clock is pretty early for a big night on the town to conclude, isn't it?"

"They were scheduled to work the next day, which meant they had to be in the fields before seven. You don't keep bankers' hours on a ranch."

"And were the men in the fields the next morning before seven, Mr. Estivar?"

"No."

"Why not?"

"I didn't get a chance to ask," Estivar said. "I never saw any of them again."

CHAPTER
FIVE

AT ELEVEN O'CLOCK Judge Gallagher called for the morning recess. His bailiff opened the massive wooden doors and people began moving out into the corridor, the elderly men on cane and crutches, the students hugging their notebooks across their chests like shields, the lady shopper, the trio of ranchers, the German woman with her bag of knitting, the ex-cop, Valenzuela, the teen-aged girl holding her baby now half-awake and fussing quietly.

Estivar, self-conscious and perspiring, rejoined his family in the last row of seats. Ysobel spoke to her husband in staccato Spanish, telling him he was a fool to admit more than he had to and answer questions that hadn't even been asked.

"I think Estivar did real good," Dulzura said. "Talking up so clear, not even nervous."

"You keep out of this," Ysobel said. "Don't interfere."

"I'm obliged to interfere. I'm his first cousin."

"Second. *Second* cousin."

"*My* mother was *his* mother's—"

"Mr. Estivar, kindly tell your second cousin, Dulzura Gonzales, not to express her opinions until they're asked for."

"I think he did real good," Dulzura repeated stubbornly. "Don't you think so, Jaime?"

Jaime looked blank, pretending not to hear, not even to be a part of this loud peculiar foreign family.

On the opposite side of the room Agnes Osborne and Devon sat silent and bewildered, like two strangers who were being tried together for a mysterious crime not described in an indictment or mentioned by a judge. No jury had been summoned to decide guilt. Guilt was assumed. It hung heavy over both the women, keeping them motionless in their seats. Devon was thirsty, she wanted to go into the corridor for a drink of water, but she had the feeling that the bailiff would follow her and that the unnamed crime she was accused of committing had canceled even so basic a right as quenching her thirst.

Mrs. Osborne was the first to speak. "I told you Estivar couldn't be trusted when the chips were down. You see what he's trying to do, don't you?"

"Not exactly."

"He's blackening our name. He's making it appear that Robert deserved whatever fate he met. All the business about prejudice, it wasn't true. Mr. Ford shouldn't have allowed him to speak lies."

"Let's go outside and take a walk in the fresh air."

"No. I must stay here and talk to Mr. Ford. He's got to straighten things out."

"What Estivar said is a matter of record. Mr. Ford or anyone else can't change it now."

"He can do *something.*"

"All right, I'll stay with you if you want me to."

"No, go take your walk."

To reach the main door Devon had to pass near the row of seats where Estivar still sat with his family. They seemed uncertain about what a recess was and how they were expected to act during it. As Devon approached, all of them, even Dulzura, looked up as though they'd forgotten about her and were surprised to see her in such a place. Then Estivar rose, and after a nudge from his father, so did Jaime.

Devon stared at the boy, thinking how much he'd grown in just the short time since she'd seen him last. Jaime must be fourteen now. When Robert was fourteen he used to follow Estivar around everywhere, he called him Tío and pestered him with questions and ate at his table. Or did he? Why had it never been mentioned to her by anyone, Robert himself, or Estivar or Agnes Osborne or Dulzura? Perhaps the man, Tío, and the boy, Robbie, and their relationship had never existed except in Estivar's mind.

She said, "Hello, Jaime."

"Hello, ma'am."

"You've been growing so fast I hardly knew you."

"Yes, ma'am."

"I haven't seen you since school started. Are you liking it better this year?"

"Yes, ma'am."

It was a polite lie, just as every answer she'd get from him would be a polite lie. The ten years' difference in their ages could have been a hundred, though it seemed only yesterday that people were telling her how

63 /

much she'd grown and asking her how she liked school.

In the corridor men and women were standing in small clusters at each window, like prisoners seeking a view of the world outside. Here and there cigarette smoke rose toward the ceiling. The teen-ager in the blond wig came out of the ladies' room. The baby was fully awake now, kicking and squirming and pulling at the girl's wig until it slipped down over her forehead and knocked off her sunglasses. Before the baby's hand was slapped away and the sunglasses and wig were put back in place, Devon had a glimpse of black hair, clipped very short, and of dark troubled eyes squinting even in the subdued light of the corridor.

"Hello, Mrs. Osborne."

"Hello."

"I guess you don't remember me, huh?"

"No."

"It's my weight, I lost fifteen pounds. Also the wig and sunglasses. Oh yeah, and the kid." She glanced down at the baby with a kind of detached interest as though she still wasn't quite sure where he'd come from. "I'm Carla, I helped Mrs. Estivar with the twins summer before last."

"Carla," Devon said. "Carla Lopez."

"Yeah, that's me. I got married for a while but it was a drag—you know? So we split and I took my real name back again. Why should I be stuck for the rest of my life with the name of a guy I hate?"

Carla Lopez, you've grown so much I hardly know you. Devon remembered a plump smiling schoolgirl hardly older than Jaime, walking down the road to meet the mailman, her thigh-high skirt emphasizing the shortness of her legs. *"Buenos días, Carla." "Good morning, Mrs. Osborne . . ."*

Carla ironing the kinks out of her long black hair in the ranch-house kitchen, with Dulzura helping her—half admiring because she'd heard this was the latest style, half reluctant because she knew Devon would eventually come to investigate the smell of scorched hair that was pervading the house. *"What on earth are you doing, you two?"* Dulzura explaining that curls and waves were no longer fashionable, while the girl knelt with her hair spread across the ironing board like a bolt of black silk . . .

Carla sitting at dusk under a tamarisk tree beside the reservoir.

"Why are you out here by yourself, Carla?"

"It's so noisy in the Estivars' house, everyone talking at once and the TV on. Last summer when I worked for the Bishops, everything was real quiet. Mr. Bishop used to read a lot and Mrs. Bishop took long walks for her headaches. She had very bad headaches."

"You'd better go inside before the mosquitoes start biting. Buenas noches."

"Good night, Mrs. Osborne."

Devon said, "Why are you here today, Carla?"

"I think it was Valenzuela's idea, he's got it in for me."

"You mean you were subpoenaed."

"Yes, I was."

"For what reason?"

"I told you, Valenzuela's got it in for me, for my whole family."

"Valenzuela has no control over subpoenas," Devon said. "He's not even a policeman any more."

"Some of the muscle stayed with him. Ask anyone in Boca de Rio—he still swaggers around like he's wearing a cop suit." She switched the baby from her right arm to her left, patting him between the shoulder blades to soothe him. "The Estivars don't like me either. Well, it's mutual, one hundred percent mutual . . . I hear Rufo got married and Cruz is in the army."

"Yes."

"It was the other one I had a crush on—Felipe. I don't suppose anyone ever hears from him."

"I wouldn't know." Devon remembered the three oldest Estivar boys only as a trio. When she used to meet them individually she was never certain whether she was seeing Cruz or Rufo or Felipe. They were uniformly quiet and polite, as though their father had spelled out to them exactly how to behave in her presence. There were rumors, passed along to her mainly by Dulzura, that away from the ranch the Estivar brothers were a great deal livelier.

Beneath the girl's platinum wig a narrow strip of brown forehead glistened with sweat. "My old lady was supposed to meet me here, she promised to look after the kid when I go on the stand. Maybe she got lost. That's the story of my life—people I count on get lost."

"I'd be glad to help if I can."

"She'll turn up sooner or later. She probably wandered into some church and started praying. She's a great prayer but it never does much good, least of all for me."

"Why not for you?"

"I got a jinx."

"Nobody believes in jinxes any more."

"No. But I got one just the same." Carla glanced down at the baby, frowning. "I hope the kid don't catch it from me. He's gonna have enough trouble without people dying all around him, disappearing, drowning, being stabbed like Mr. Osborne."

"Mr. Osborne didn't die because of your jinx."

"Well, I feel like if it wasn't for me he'd still be alive. And her, too."

"Yes?"

"Mrs. Bishop. She drowned."

Mrs. Bishop had bad headaches and took long walks and drowned.

THE TABLE RESERVED for the press when court was in session had been vacated for recess. Across its polished mahogany surface Ford and Mrs. Osborne faced each other. Mrs. Osborne still wore her public face and her jaunty blue hat, but Ford was beginning to look irritable and his soft voice had developed a rasp.

"I repeat, Mrs. Osborne, Estivar talked more freely than I anticipated. No harm was done, however."

"Not to you, nothing touches you. But what about me? All that talk about prejudice and ill-feeling, it was embarrassing."

"Murder is an embarrassing business. There's no law stating the mother of the victim will be spared."

"I refuse to believe that a murder occurred."

"O.K., O.K., you have a right to your opinion. But as far as this hearing today is concerned, your son is dead."

"All the more reason why you shouldn't have allowed Estivar to blacken his name."

"I let him talk," Ford said, "just as I intend to let the rest of the witnesses talk. This Judge Gallagher is no dope. He'd be highly suspicious if I tried to present Robert as a perfect young man without an enemy in the world. Perfect young men don't get murdered, they don't even get born. In presenting the background of a murder, the victim's faults are more pertinent than his virtues, his enemies are more important than his friends. If Robert wasn't getting along well with Estivar, if he had trouble with the migrant workers or with his neighbors—"

"The only neighbors he ever had the slightest trouble with were the Bishops. You surely wouldn't dredge that up again—Ruth's been dead for nearly two years."

"And Robert had no part in her death?"

"Of course not." She shook her head, and the hat jumped forward as though it meant to peck at a tormentor. "Robert tried to help her. She was a very unhappy woman."

"Why?"

"Because he was kind."

"No. I meant, why was she unhappy?"

"Perhaps because Leo—Mr. Bishop—was more interested in his crops than he was in his wife. She was lonely. She used to come over and talk to Robert. That's all there was between them, talk. She was old enough to be his mother. He felt sorry for her, she was such a pathetic little thing."

"Is that what he told you?"

"He didn't have to tell me. It was obvious. Day after day she dragged her trouble over to our house like a sick animal she couldn't cure, couldn't kill."

"How did she get to your house?"

"Walked. She liked to pretend that she did it for the exercise, but of course no one was fooled, not even Leo." She paused, running a gloved hand across the surface of the table as though testing it for dirt. "I suppose you know how she died."

"Yes. I looked it up in the newspaper files. She was attempting to cross the river during a winter rain, got caught by a flash flood and drowned. A coroner's jury returned a verdict of accidental death. There were indications that she suffered from despondency, but suicide was ruled out by the finding of her suitcase a mile or so downstream, waterlogged but still intact. It was packed for a journey. She was going some place."

"Perhaps."

"Why just 'perhaps,' Mrs. Osborne?"

"There was no evidence to prove Ruth and the suitcase entered the water at the same time. It's easy enough to pack a woman's suitcase and toss it in a river, especially for someone with access to her belongings."

"Like a husband?"

"Like a husband."

"Why would a husband do that?"

"To make people think his wife was on her way to meet another man and run away with him. The easiest method of avoiding blame is to cast it on someone else. That suitcase turned Leo into a poor grieving widower and Robert into an irresponsible seducer."

"What was in it?"

"You mean exactly?"

"Yes."

"I don't know. What difference does it make?"

"A woman preparing for a rendezvous with her lover wouldn't pack quite the same things as a man would pack for her, even a husband. I presume the contents of the suitcase were exhibited at the coroner's inquest."

"I didn't attend the inquest. By that time I'd stopped going anywhere because of the gossip. Oh, nothing was ever said in front of Robert or me, but it was there on everyone's face, even the people who worked for us. If she hadn't died it would have been laughable, the idea of Robert running off with a woman twice his age, a pale skinny little thing who looked like an elderly child."

"What do you think happened to Ruth Bishop, Mrs. Osborne?"

"I know what didn't happen. She did not pack a suitcase and start across that river in order to keep a rendezvous with my son. It was raining before she left the house, and she was well aware of the danger of a flash flood."

"You believe that she walked into the river deliberately?"

"Perhaps."

"And that Leo Bishop packed a suitcase and put it into the water so it would be found later downstream."

"Again, perhaps."

"Why?"

"A wife's suicide puts her husband in a bad light, starts people asking questions and prying under surfaces. As it was, all the bad light was on us. I sent Robert on a trip East to give the scandal a chance to blow over. That's where he met Devon and married her two weeks later. Funny how things repeat themselves, isn't it? The first thing that struck me about Devon was how much she looked like Ruth Bishop."

People had begun returning to the courtroom: the high school students; Leo Bishop and the ranchers; the Estivars, with Lum Wing shuffling along behind like a family pet that was currently out of favor; Carla Lopez, freshly groomed and without her baby, as though she'd suddenly decided she was too young to be burdened with a child and had left it somewhere in the corridor or the ladies' room.

Ford's only reaction to the people coming back in was a slight lowering of his voice.

"You also sent Robert away after his father's death, is that right?"

"Yes."

"How did his father die, Mrs. Osborne?"

"I've already told you."

"Tell me again."

"He fell off a tractor and fractured his skull. He was in a coma for days."

"And after his death Robert was enrolled in a school in Arizona."

"I was depressed and poor company for a growing boy. Robert needed men to guide him."

"Estivar claims that the guidance was the wrong kind."

"He exaggerates. Most Mexicans do."

"Do you agree with Estivar that Robert had changed when he returned home?"

"Of course he'd changed. They're years of change, between fifteen and seventeen. Robert went away a boy and came back a man who had to take over the management of a ranch. I repeat, Estivar exaggerates. The relationship between him and Robert was never as close as he likes to remember it. Why should it have been? Robert had a perfectly good father of his own."

"And they were on friendly terms?"

"Of course."

"How did Mr. Osborne fall off the tractor, Mrs. Osborne?"

"I wasn't there when it happened. And my husband didn't tell me because he never regained consciousness. Just what are you trying to prove anyway? First, you bring up Ruth Bishop's death and now my husband's. They were totally unconnected and half a dozen years apart."

"I didn't bring up the subject of Ruth Bishop," Ford said. "You did."

"You led me into it."

"By the way, it's not exactly easy to fall off a tractor."

"I wouldn't know. I've never tried."

"The rumor is that your husband was drunk."

"So I heard."

"Was he?"

"An autopsy was performed. There was nothing in the report about alcohol."

"You said a minute ago that Mr. Osborne lay in a coma for days. All traces of alcohol would have disappeared from the bloodstream during that time."

"I'm not a doctor. How would I know?"

"I think you know a great deal, Mrs. Osborne. The problem is getting you to admit it."

"That was an ungentlemanly remark."

"I come from a long line of ungentlemen," Ford said. "You'd better go back to your place. The recess is over."

Judge Gallagher was striding back into the courtroom, his black robe flapping around him like the broken wings of a raven.

"Remain seated and come to order," the clerk said. "Superior Court is now in session."

71 /

CHAPTER
SIX

THE NAME OF JOHN LOOMIS was called, and one of the men in ranchers' clothes came to the witness box and was sworn in: John Sylvester Loomis, 514 Paloverde Street, Boca de Rio; occupation, doctor of veterinary medicine. Dr. Loomis testified that on the morning of October 13, 1967, he was asleep in the apartment above his place of business when he was awakened by someone pounding on the office door. He went downstairs and found Robert Osborne with his dog, Maxie, on a leash.

"I gave him hell, if you'll pardon the expression, for

waking me up so early, since I'd been at a foaling until three o'clock. But he seemed to think it was urgent, that someone had poisoned his dog."

"What was your opinion?"

"I saw no evidence of poison. The dog was lively, his eyes were clear and bright, nose cold, no offensive breath odor. Mr. Osborne said he'd found Maxie in a field before dawn, that the dog's legs were twitching violently, it was frothing at the mouth and had lost control of its bowels. I persuaded Mr. Osborne to leave the dog with me for a few hours, and he said he'd pick it up on his way home from San Diego in the late afternoon or early evening."

"And did he?"

"Yes. About seven o'clock that night."

"Meanwhile you'd had a chance to examine the dog."

"Yes."

"And what did you find out?"

"Nothing absolutely positive. But I was pretty sure it had suffered an epileptic seizure. Such seizures are not uncommon in dogs as they get older, and spaniels like Maxie are particularly susceptible. Once a seizure is over, the dog makes an immediate and complete recovery. It's the speed of the recovery, in fact, which helps with the diagnosis."

"Did you explain this to Mr. Osborne, Dr. Loomis?"

"I made an attempt. But he had this thing in his mind about poison, that the dog had been poisoned."

"Was there any basis for his belief?"

"None that I could see," Loomis said. "I didn't argue with him, though. It seemed a touchy subject."

"Why?"

"People often identify with their pets. I got the impression that Mr. Osborne thought someone was trying to poison *him.*"

"Thank you, Dr. Loomis. You may step down now."

Leo Bishop was called as the next witness. His reluctance to take the stand was evidenced by the slowness of his movements and the look of apology he gave Devon as he passed her. When he responded to Ford's questions about his name and address, his voice was so low that even the court reporter, who was sitting directly below the witness box, had to ask him to speak up.

Ford said, "Would you please repeat that, Mr. Bishop?"

"Leo James Bishop."

"And the address?"

"Rancho Obispo."

"You are the owner as well as the operator of the ranch?"

"Yes."

"What's the location of your ranch in relation to the Osborne ranch?"

"It's just to the east and southeast, with the river as the boundary line."

"In fact, you and the Osbornes are next-door neighbors."

"You might put it like that, though it's a long way between doors." *A long way and a river.*

"You knew Robert Osborne, of course."

"Yes."

"Had known him for many years."

"Yes."

"Will you tell the court when and where you last saw him, Mr. Bishop?"

"On the morning of October 13, 1967, in town."

"The town of Boca de Rio."

"Yes."

"Would you explain the circumstances of that meeting?"

"One of my green-carders showed up for work suffering from stomach cramps. I was afraid his symptoms might be the result of an insecticide we'd used the previous day, so I drove him into Boca to a doctor. On the way I saw

Robert's car parked on Main Street outside a café. He was standing on the curb talking to a young woman."

"Did you honk your horn or wave at him, anything like that?"

"No. He seemed busy, I didn't want to interrupt. Besides, I had a sick man in the car."

"Still, it would have been the natural thing to do, taking a second or two to greet a close friend."

"He wasn't a close friend," Leo said quietly. "There was a generation between us. And some old trouble."

"Would this 'old trouble' have any bearing on the present case?"

"I don't think so."

Ford pretended to consult the pages of yellow foolscap on the table in front of him, giving himself time to decide whether to pursue the subject further or whether it would be wiser to stick to the main theme he'd chosen to present. Overkill might be a mistake in view of Judge Gallagher's skeptical mind. He said, "Mr. Bishop, you've been present in the courtroom all morning, have you not?"

"Yes."

"So you heard Mr. Estivar testify that he hired a crew of Mexicans to work on the Osborne ranch at the end of September, and that these men disappeared on the night of October 13 . . . As a grower you're familiar with the pirating of work crews, are you not, Mr. Bishop?"

"Yes."

"In fact, in the summer of 1965 you had occasion to report that a crew which you'd hired to pick melons had disappeared during the night following a payday."

"That's correct."

"Now, on the surface, what happened to your crew and what happened to Mr. Estivar's crew appeared to be similar. There was, however, an important difference, was there not?"

"Yes. My men were located by noon the next day. A

grower near Chula Vista had simply convinced them they could do better at his place, so they left. But the men from the Osborne ranch were never found. Chances are they crossed the border before the police even knew a crime had been committed."

"When did you learn that a crime had been committed, Mr. Bishop?"

"I was awakened about one-thirty in the morning by a deputy from the sheriff's department. He said Robert Osborne was missing and the surrounding ranches were being searched for traces of him."

"What did you do then?"

"I got dressed and joined the search. At least I tried to. The deputy in charge sent me back in the house."

"What was his name?"

"Valenzuela."

"Why did he refuse your offer of assistance?"

"He said a lot of searches had been messed up by amateurs and this wasn't going to be one of them if he could help it."

"All right, thank you, Mr. Bishop. You are excused."

Ford waited until Leo returned to his place in the spectators' section, then asked the clerk to call Carla Lopez to the stand.

Carla rose and walked slowly to the front of the room. In the hot dry air her pink and yellow nylon shift clung to her moist body like a magnet. If she was embarrassed or nervous she managed to conceal the fact. Her voice was bored when she took the oath, and the huge round sunglasses gave her an Orphan Annie look of complete blankness.

"State your name, please," Ford said.

"Carla Dolores Lopez."

"Miss or Mrs.?"

"Miss. I'm getting a divorce, so I took back my maiden name."

"Where do you live, Miss Lopez?"

"431 Catalpa Street, San Diego, Apartment 9."

"Are you employed?"

"I quit my job last week. I'm looking for something better."

"Did you know Robert Osborne, Miss Lopez?"

"Yes."

"A few minutes ago Mr. Bishop testified that he saw Mr. Osborne on the morning of October 13 talking to a young woman outside a café in Boca de Rio. Were you that young woman?"

"Yes."

"Who initiated the conversation?"

"What do you mean by that?"

"Who started talking first?"

"He did. I was just walking along the street by myself when he pulled up to the curb beside me and asked if he could speak to me for a minute. I had nothing better to do, so I said yes."

"What did Mr. Osborne talk to you about, Miss Lopez?"

"My brothers," Carla said. "They used to work for him, my two older brothers, and Mr. Osborne wanted to know if they might want to come and work for him again."

"Did he give any reason?"

"He said the last crew Estivar had hired was no good, they had no experience, and he needed someone like my brothers to show them how things were done. I told him my brothers wouldn't be caught dead doing that kind of labor no more. They didn't have to squat and stoop like monkeys, they had respectable stand-up jobs in a gas station."

"Did Mr. Osborne make any further remarks about the crew he had working for him?"

"No."

"He gave no indication, for instance, that he suspected they might have entered the country without papers?"

"No."

"Did he use the terms wetback, *mojado* or *alambre?*"

"Not that I remember. The rest of the talk was personal
—you know, like between he and I."

The girl's long silver-painted fingernails scratched at
her throat as if they were trying to ease an itch deep inside
and out of reach. It was her first sign of nervousness.

"Was there anything in the conversation," Ford said,
"which might have bearing on the present hearing?"

"I don't think so. He asked me about my baby—I wasn't
showing yet but the whole town knew about it, it being
that kind of town—and he said his wife was having a baby
too. He seemed kind of jumpy about it. Could be he was
scared it would turn out like him."

"What do you mean by that?"

"Well, there was a lot of gossip about him when Mrs.
Bishop drowned. Maybe some of it was true. Or maybe he
just had a jinx like me. I'm an expert on jinxes. I've had one
ever since I was born."

"Indeed."

"For instance, if I did a rain dance there'd probably be
a year's drought or even a snowstorm."

"The court must deal in facts, Miss Lopez, not jinxes
and rain dances."

"You have your facts," the girl said. "I have mine."

CHAPTER
SEVEN

THE EXODUS from the courtroom for lunch was faster and more complete than it had been for the morning recess. Devon waited until only the bailiff remained.

He glanced at her curiously. "This room is locked up during the noon hour, ma'am."

"Oh. Thank you."

"If you're not feeling well, there's a ladies' lounge in the basement where you can get coffee and things like that."

"I'm all right."

Agnes Osborne had driven back to her apartment to rest, suffering more from weariness than from hunger. With her out of the way Devon thought Leo might be waiting for her in the corridor and they would have lunch together. But there was no sign of him. The corridor was deserted except for a pair of tourists taking pictures out of one of the barred windows and, in an alcove beyond a row of telephone booths, the ex-policeman, Valenzuela, talking to a short stout Mexican woman who was holding a baby on her left arm. The child was sucking on a pacifier and regarding Valenzuela with mild interest.

Valenzuela, so dapper earlier in the day, had begun to show the effects of the increasing heat and tension. He'd taken off his coat and tie and under each arm of his striped shirt there was a dark semicircle like a stain of secret guilt. When Devon approached he looked at her with disapproval, as though she were someone from a remote corner of his past and had no right to be popping up in the present without warning or permission.

As she walked by she nodded but didn't speak. Everything had been said between them: *"I've done what I could, Mrs. Osborne. Searched the fields, dragged the reservoir, walked up and down the riverbed. But there are a hundred more fields, a dozen more reservoirs, miles and miles of riverbed." "You must try again, try harder." "It's no use. I think they took him into Mexico."* The following spring Valenzuela phoned Devon and told her he'd quit his job in the sheriff's office and was now selling insurance. He asked her if she wanted to buy any and she said no, very politely . . .

A few blocks from the courthouse she found a small hamburger stand. She sat at a table hardly bigger than a handkerchief and ordered a burger with French fries. The odor of stale grease, the ketchup bottle with its darkening dribble, the thin round patty of meat identical to ones she'd eaten in Philadelphia, New Haven, Boston—they were all so normal and familiar, they made her feel like an ordinary girl who ate lunch at hamburger stands and had no business with bailiffs or judges. She ate slowly, prolonging her stay in the little place, her role of ordinary girl.

After lunch she began her reluctant return to the courthouse, pausing now and then to stare out at the sea. *"I think they took him into Mexico,"* Valenzuela had said. *"Or maybe dumped him in the sea and a high tide will bring him in."* A hundred high tides came and went before Devon stopped hoping; Mrs. Osborne had never stopped. Devon knew she still carried a tide table in her purse, still walked for miles along the beaches every week, her eye on specks in the water that turned out to be buoys or harbor seals, pelagic birds or pieces of floating lumber. *"In salt water this cold it would take a week or two for gases to form in the tissues and bring a body to the surface."* The first week passed, and the second, and fifty more. *"Not everything that goes into the sea comes out again, Mrs. Osborne."* With each tide things floated into shore and were stranded on the beach—driftwood, jellyfish, shark eggs, oil-soaked grebes and cormorants and scoters, lobster traps, plastic bottles, odd shoes and other pieces of clothing. Every scrap of the clothing was collected and taken to a room in the basement of the sheriff's department to be dried out and examined. None of it belonged to Robert.

Devon turned away from the sea and quickened her pace. It was then that she spotted Estivar. He was sitting alone on a bus-stop bench under a silver dollar tree. At the slightest stirring of air the silver discs of leaves twitched and jumped, eager to be spent. Their quick gay movements altered the lights and shadows, so that Estivar's face from a distance appeared very lively. As she drew closer she saw that it was no livelier than the concrete bench. He rose slowly at her approach, as though he was sorry to see her.

She said, "Aren't you having lunch, Estivar?"

"Later. The others wanted a picnic at the zoo, they left me a sandwich and an avocado. Will you sit down, Mrs. Osborne?"

"Yes, thanks." As she sat down she wondered if the bench had been made of concrete because it was a durable material or because its cold roughness would discourage people from remaining too long. "Don't you like the park?"

"Live things shouldn't be put in cages. I prefer to watch the sea. All that water, think what we could do at the ranch with all that water . . . Where is Mrs. Osborne?"

"She went home to rest for a while."

"I know she resented some of the things I said on the stand this morning. But I couldn't help it, they were true, I was under oath. What did she expect from me? Probably some of those nice lies she believes herself."

"You mustn't be too hard on her, Estivar."

"Why not? She's too hard on me. I heard her at recess this morning talking to the lawyer. I heard her clear across the room speaking my name like a dirty word. What's she got against me? I kept that place going for her when her son was too young to be any help and her husband was too —" He drew in his breath sharply, as though someone had given him a warning poke in the stomach.

"Too what?"

"He's dead, it doesn't matter any more."

"It does to me."

"I thought you'd have found out on your own by this time."

"I only know he died by accident."

"That was the verdict."

"Didn't you agree with it?"

"If you go around looking for accidents, asking for them, they can't be called accidents any more. Mr. Osborne's 'accident' happened before ten o'clock in the

morning, and he'd already drunk enough bourbon to para-
lyze an ordinary man." Estivar spread his hands in a little
gesture of despair. "It wasn't a case of bad luck killing him
when he was just forty-three years old, it was a case of
good luck keeping him alive that long."

"When did he become an alcoholic?"

"I'm not sure. Between the two of them they managed
to keep it secret for years. But eventually it reached a point
where a new crew would take one look at him and label
him a *borrachín.*"

"Is that why Robert spent so much time with you as he
was growing up?"

"Yes. He'd come over to my house when things got too
rough. I didn't say any of this on the witness stand, naturally, but I told Mr. Ford last week. He was asking me a lot
of questions about the Osbornes. I had to tell him the truth.
I knew she wouldn't, she never told anyone. She had this
game she played. If Mr. Osborne was too drunk to come
out and work, she said he had a touch of flu or a migraine
or a toothache or a sprained back. Once he had to be
carried in from the fields, out cold and reeking of whiskey,
but she claimed he must have suffered a heat stroke,
though it was a winter day with a pale cool little sun. She
couldn't bring herself to admit the truth even while she
was hiring my boy, Rufo, to haul away the bottles every
week." He raised his head, frowning up at the round silver
leaves as though they represented the dollars and half-
dollars Rufo had been paid to dispose of the bottles. "It
was silly, the whole cover-up business, but you couldn't
help admire how hard she worked at it and what guts it
took, especially when he got quarrelsome."

"How did she handle him then?"

"Oh, she tried lots of things, same as any woman married to a drunk. But eventually she developed a routine.
She'd maneuver him into the living room one way or another, close the doors and windows and pull the drapes.

Then the arguing would start. If things got too loud she'd sit down at that piano of hers and start playing to cover them up, a piece with good firm chords like 'March of the Toreadors.' She couldn't admit that they quarreled any more than she could admit that he drank. Everybody caught on, of course. Even the men working around the place, when they heard that piano, they'd look at each other and grin."

"What about Robert?"

"Lots of the arguing was about him and how he should be brought up, disciplined, educated, trained. But they would have argued even if the boy had never been born. He was just a peg to hang things on. When he got older, ten or eleven, I tried to explain this to him. I told him he hadn't caused the trouble and he couldn't stop it, so he might as well learn to live with it."

"How could a ten-year-old understand such a thing?"

"I think he did. Anyway, he used to show up at my place when he sensed trouble on the way. Sometimes he didn't make it in time and he'd be caught between the two of them. One day I heard the piano music start in real loud and I waited and waited for Robbie to show up. Finally I went over to the ranch house to find out what was happening. She had forgotten to pull the drapes across a side window and I could see the three of them inside the room. She was at the piano, with Robbie sitting on the bench beside her looking sick and scared. Mr. Osborne was propped up against the mantel, the veins in his neck sticking out like ropes. His mouth was moving, so was hers. But all I could hear was the bang bang bang of that piano, loud enough to wake the dead. 'Onward, Christian Soldiers.' "

"What do you mean?"

"That's what she was playing, over and over, 'Onward, Christian Soldiers.' It seems funny now, her using a hymn. But it wasn't funny then. That fight was the same as all the others, long and mean and deadly, the kind nobody can win, so everybody loses, especially the innocent. I wanted to get Robbie out of that room and away from that house until things quieted down. I went inside and started pounding on the living-room door as hard as I could. A minute or so later the piano stopped and Mrs. Osborne opened the door. 'Oh, Estivar,' she said, 'we were just having a little concert.' I asked her if Robbie could come over and help my son, Cruz, with his homework. She said, 'Certainly. I don't think Robbie cares much for music anyway . . .' Sometimes when I wake up in the night I swear I can hear the sound of that piano, though it isn't even there any more, I helped the movers take it out of the house myself."

"Why are you telling me all this?"

"No one else will, and it's time you knew."

"I didn't want to know."

"You wanted to know more than I wanted to tell you, Mrs. Osborne, especially today. But who can be sure? I may not get another chance to talk to you like this."

"You sound as if something is going to happen."

"Something always does."

"The ranch will remain the same," she said. "And you'll continue on as foreman. I don't plan on changing anything."

"Life is something that happens to you while you're making other plans. I read that somewhere, and it's like the piano music, it keeps running through my mind. Robbie's life was planned—high school, college, a profession. Then his father fell off a tractor and things changed before they had a chance to begin."

A silence fell between them, emphasized by the noise all around: the roar of freeway traffic and planes landing and taking off from Lindbergh Field and from the Naval Air Station across the bay. At the top of a palm tree nearby a mockingbird had begun to sing. It was October, the wrong time to be singing, but the bird sang anyway, with loud delight, and Estivar's face softened at the sound.

"*Sinsonte,*" he said. "Listen."

"A mockingbird?"

"Yes."

"Why is he singing now?"

"He wants to—that's reason enough for a bird."

"Maybe he thinks it's spring."

"Maybe."

"Lucky bird."

A carillon began chiming the first quarter of an hour. Estivar rose quickly. "It's time I went and picked up my family."

"You didn't eat your sandwich."

"I'll have a chance in the car."

She rose too. Her eyes felt hot and dry and tired, as though they'd seen too much too quickly and needed a rest in some quiet sunless place.

"I'm sorry I had to tell you things you didn't want to know," he said.

"You were right, of course. I need all the information I can get in order to make sensible plans."

"Yes, Mrs. Osborne." *Life, Mrs. Osborne, is what happens to you while you are making sensible plans.*

She began walking slowly back to the courthouse as if by delaying her return she could delay the proceeding and the verdict. There was no doubt in her mind what the verdict would be. Robert, who had died a dozen times to the strains of "Onward, Christian Soldiers" and "March of the Toreadors," would die this time to the tuneless hum of strangers and the occasional beat of a gavel.

CHAPTER
EIGHT

COURT RECONVENED ten minutes late because Judge Gallagher was caught in a traffic jam on the way back from his club. Even with this extra time allowance Agnes Osborne, scheduled to be the first witness of the afternoon, was still absent at one forty-five. A conference was held at the bench and it was decided not to delay the proceeding further by waiting for Mrs. Osborne but to call the next witness.

"Dulzura Gonzales."

Dulzura heard her name but she didn't respond until

Jaime jabbed her in the side with his elbow. "Hey, that's you."

"I know it's me."

"Well, hurry up."

Already breathless from fear Dulzura had trouble getting to her feet and out into the aisle; and once she was in motion she walked too rapidly, so that her giant dress swirled around her like a tent fighting a storm.

"Do you swear that the testimony you are about to give in the matter now pending before this court shall be the truth, the whole truth, and nothing but the truth?"

She swore. Her hand left moist prints on the wooden railing around the witness box.

"State your full name, please," Ford said.

"Dulzura Ynez Maria Amata Gonzales."

"Miss or Mrs.?"

"Miss." Her nervous giggle swept through the room, raising little gusts of laughter and a flurry of doubt.

"Where do you live, Miss Gonzales?"

"The same place as the others—you know, the Osborne ranch."

"What do you do there?"

"Well, lots of things."

"I meant, what are you paid to do, Miss Gonzales?"

"Cook and laundry, mostly. A little cleaning now and then."

"How long have you worked for the Osbornes?"

"Seven years."

"Who hired you?"

"Mrs. Osborne, Senior. There wasn't anybody but her around. Mr. Osborne was dead and the boy away at school. My first cousin, Estivar, gave me a nice recommend on a piece of paper."

"Miss Gonzales, I want you to try and recall the evening of October the thirteenth last year."

"I don't have to try. I recall it already."

"There were special circumstances that fixed the day in your memory?"

"Yes, sir. It was my birthday. Usually I get time off to celebrate, maybe go into Boca with a couple of the boys after work. But that day I couldn't, it was Friday the thirteenth. I'm not allowed to leave the house on Friday the thirteenth."

"Not allowed?"

"A *quiromántico* told me never to because of strange lines in my hands. So I just stayed home like it was no special day and cooked dinner and served it."

"At what time?"

"About seven-thirty, later than usual on account of Mr. Osborne had been to the city."

"Did you see Mr. Osborne after dinner?"

"Yes, sir. He came out to the kitchen while I was cleaning up. He said he forgot to buy my birthday present, like Mrs. Osborne asked him to, and would I accept money, and I said I sure would."

"Was Mr. Osborne wearing his spectacles when he came out to the kitchen?"

"No, sir. But he could see O.K., so I guess he was wearing those little pieces of glass over his eyeballs."

"Contact lenses."

"Yes."

"What did he give you for your birthday, Miss Gonzales?"

"A twenty-dollar bill."

"Did he take the bill from his wallet in your presence?"

"Yes, sir."

"Did you notice anything of interest about the wallet?"

"It was full of money. I never saw Mr. Osborne's wallet before and I was surprised and kind of worried too. The boys don't get much pay."

"Boys?"

"The workers that come and go."

"The migrants?"

"Yes. It would of been a real temptation to them if they found out how much money Mr. Osborne was carrying."

"Thank you, Miss Gonzales. You may—"

"I'm not saying any of them did it, killed him for the money. I'm just saying that a lot of money is a big temptation to a poor man."

"We understand that, Miss Gonzales. Thank you ... Will Mr. Lum Wing take the stand, please?"

Lum Wing, encouraged by his sunny hour in the park, gave his name in a high clear voice with a trace of southern accent.

"Where do you live, Mr. Wing?"

"Sometimes here, sometimes there. Where the work is."

"You have a permanent address, don't you?"

"When there's nothing better to do I stay at my daughter's house in Boca de Rio. She's got six kids, I share a room with two of my grandsons, I keep away from there as much as possible."

"What is your profession, Mr. Wing?"

"I used to be cook with a circus. What my daughter tells the neighbors, I retired. What happened, the circus went bust."

"You come out of retirement and take a job now and then?"

"Yes, sir, to get out of the house."

"Your work has brought you to the Osborne ranch at various times?"

"Yes."

"You're working there now, in fact?"

"Yes, sir."

"And you were there a year ago, on October 13?"

"Yes."

"Where do you stay when you're working at the ranch?"

Lum Wing described his living arrangements in the curtained-off corner of the former barn that served as a mess hall. In the late afternoon of October 13 he had cooked supper as usual. After the men departed for their payday fling in Boca de Rio he'd drawn his curtain, set up a chess game and opened a bottle of wine. The wine made him sleepy, so he lay down on his cot. He must have dozed off, because the next thing he remembered was the sound of voices speaking loud and fast in Spanish on the other side of the curtain. On occasion other basic needs besides eating were satisfied at the mess-hall tables and Lum Wing made it a habit to ignore what went on. Moving quietly in the darkness he checked his case of knives, his pocket watch and chess set, the rest of the bottle of wine, and finally the money belt he wore even when sleeping. Finding everything intact he returned to his cot. The voices continued.

"Did you recognize any of them?" Ford asked.

After a moment's hesitation Lum Wing shook his head.

"Did you hear what they were saying?"

"They talked too fast. Also I didn't listen."

"Do you understand Spanish, Mr. Wing?"

"Four, five words."

"I gather that you didn't overhear any of those four or five words spoken on that occasion?"

"I'm an old man. I mind my own business. I don't listen, I don't hear, I don't get in trouble."

"There was a great deal of trouble that night, Mr. Wing. You must have heard some of it whether you listened or not. You appear to have normal hearing for a man your age."

"I fix it so it's not so normal." He showed the court how he made earplugs out of little pieces of paper. "Beside the plugs, there was the wine. It made me sleepy. Also I was tired. I work hard, up before five every morning, doing this, doing that."

"All right, Mr. Wing, I believe you . . . You've been employed at the Osborne ranch quite a few times, haven't you?"

"Six, seven."

"Did Robert Osborne speak Spanish?"

"Not to me." Lum Wing stared blandly up at the ceiling.

"Well, did you ever hear him speak to the men in Spanish?"

"Maybe two, three times."

"And maybe oftener? A lot oftener?"

"Maybe."

"It would, in fact, have been quite possible for you to recognize Mr. Osborne's voice even if he was talking in a foreign language?"

"I wouldn't like to say that. I don't want to make trouble."

"The trouble is made, Mr. Wing."

"It could be worse."

"Not for Robert Osborne."

"There were others," the old man said, blinking. "Other people. Mr. Osborne wasn't talking to himself. Why would he talk to himself in Spanish?"

"Then you did recognize Mr. Osborne's voice that night?"

"Maybe. I'm not swearing to it."

"Mr. Wing, we have reason to believe that a fight which ended in a murder took place in the same room in which you claim to have been sleeping. Do you realize that?"

"I didn't commit a murder, I didn't commit a fight. I was sleeping innocent as a baby with my earplugs in until Mr. Estivar woke me up by shaking my arm and shining a flashlight in my face. I said what happened? And he said what happened, Mr. Osborne is missing and there's blood all over the floor and the cops are on their way."

"What did you do then, Mr. Wing?"

"Put on my pants."

"You got dressed."

"Same thing."

"I take it that your earplugs had been removed by this time."

"Yes, sir."

"And you could hear perfectly well?"

"Yes, sir."

"What did you hear, Mr. Wing?"

"Nothing. I thought funny thing how quiet, where is everybody, and I look out my window. I see lights on all over the ranch, the main house, Estivar's place, the garage where they keep the heavy machinery, the bunkhouse, even in some of the tamarisk trees around the reservoir. I think again what's the matter, all those lights and no noise. Then I see the big truck is gone, the one the men came in, and the bunkhouse is empty."

"What time was that, Mr. Wing?"

"I don't know."

"You mentioned previously that you had a pocket watch."

"I never thought to look at it. I was scared, I wanted to get out of that place."

"And did you?"

"I opened my door—there are two doors to the building, the front one the men use and the back one that's mine. I stepped outside. Estivar's oldest son, Cruz, was standing between me and the bunkhouse with a rifle over his shoulder."

"Did you speak to him?"

"He spoke to me. He told me to go back inside and stay there, because the police were on their way and when they asked me if I touched anything I better be able to say no. So I sat on the edge of my cot, then in five, ten minutes the police arrived."

There was a sudden audible stirring throughout the

courtroom, as if the arrival of the police marked the end of a period of tension and gave people freedom to move. They coughed, changed position, whispered to their neighbors, sighed, stretched, yawned.

Ford waited for the sounds to subside. Without actually turning to face the audience he could see that the place where Agnes Osborne had sat during the morning was still empty. His uneasiness over her absence was tinged with guilt. He had probably talked to her too harshly. Women like Mrs. Osborne, who were blunt themselves and seemed to invite bluntness from others, were often the least able to tolerate it.

Ford said, "What happened after the police arrived, Mr. Wing?"

"Plenty, plenty of noise, cars moving around, doors banging, people talking and shouting. Pretty soon one of the deputies came to me and started asking questions like what you asked, did I see anything, did I hear anything. But mostly he wanted to know about my knives."

"Knives, Mr. Wing?"

"I carry my own knives to cook with—cleaver, choppers, parers, slicers, carver. I keep them clean and sharp, locked up in a case and the key in my money belt. I opened the case and showed him they were all there, nothing stolen."

"Did you ever hear of a butterfly knife?"

Lum Wing's impassive face looked as surprised as possible. "A knife to cut *butterflies?*"

"No. It's one that resembles a butterfly when the blade is open."

"I leave such silly things to the Mexicans. Around here they all carry knives, the fancier the better, like jewelry."

"When the deputy questioned you that night, you were not able to give him any more information than you have given the court this afternoon?"

"No, no more."

"Thank you, Mr. Wing. You may return to your seat ...
Will Jaime Estivar come to the stand, please?"

As they met in the aisle the old man and the young one
exchanged glances of puzzlement and resignation: it was
a middle-aged world, which Lum Wing had passed and
Jaime hadn't yet reached and neither of them cared about
or understood.

CHAPTER
NINE

"FOR THE RECORD," Ford said, "would you state your name, please?"

"My church name or my school name?"

"Is there a difference?"

"Yes, sir. I was christened with five names, but at school I just use Jaime Estivar because otherwise I'd take up too much room on report cards and attendance sheets, things like that." He had sworn to tell the truth, but the very first thing he uttered was a lie. What's more, it tripped off his tongue without a moment's hesitation. The boys he admired at school were called Chris, Pete, Tim, or sometimes Smith, McGregor, Foster, Jones; he couldn't afford to have them find out he was really Jaime Ricardo Salvador Luis Hermano Estivar.

"Your school name will be sufficient," Ford said.

"Jaime Estivar."

"How old are you, Jaime?"

"Fourteen."

"And you live with your family at the Osborne ranch?"

"Yes, sir."

"Tell us about your family, Jaime."

"Well, uh, I don't know what's to tell." He glanced down at his parents and Dulzura and Lum Wing, seeking inspiration. He found none. "I mean, they're just a family, no big deal or anything."

"Do you have brothers and sisters?"

"Yes, sir. Three of each."

"Are they living at home?"

"Only me and my two younger sisters, they're twins. My oldest brother, Cruz, is with the army in Korea. Rufo is married and lives in Salinas. Felipe's got a good job in an aircraft plant in Seattle. He sent me ten dollars for Christmas and fifteen for my birthday."

"When your brothers were at home, they all had chores to do around the ranch, did they?"

"Yes, sir."

"What about you?"

"I help after school and on weekends."

"Do you get paid?"

"Yes, sir."

"How?"

"My pop just hands me the money and says go buy yourself a Cadillac."

"What I meant was, do you get paid by the hour or by the job?"

"The job usually. Also for the last three years I've been in business for myself part of the time. Pumpkins."

"You're pretty young to be in business for yourself."

"Well, I don't make much money," Jaime said earnestly.

Ford smiled. "How do you go about getting in the pumpkin business, Jaime?"

"I just took over from Felipe, the way he did from Rufo and Rufo from Cruz. It all started with old Mr. Osborne lending Cruz a field for a crop that would bring him money to put away for his education. Cruz and Rufo grew a lot of different things. It was Felipe who thought of pumpkins. They grow fast and don't take much work and you harvest them all at once at the beginning of October."

"And is this what you did at the beginning of October, 1967?"

"Yes, sir."

"After the pumpkins were picked and sold, you plowed the vines under?"

"I did when my dad said I'd better get to it or else."

"What date was that?"

"Saturday morning, November 4, three weeks after Mr. Osborne disappeared. The vines were drying up by that time and a lot of them were broken and, you know, trampled down by people looking for clues and stuff like that."

"Did anyone find any 'clues and stuff like that'?"

"I don't think so, not in the pumpkin field."

"Did you?"

"I found the knife," Jaime said. "The butterfly knife."

"Where was it in the field?"

"The southwest corner."

"The corner nearest the road leading out of the ranch?"

"Yes, sir."

"Was it buried in the ground?"

"No, sir. It looked like maybe somebody flung it out of a car window to get rid of it and it sort of stuck in the ground underneath one of the vines."

"I'm going to show you a knife and ask you if it is the

one you found." Ford held up the knife, now labeled with an identification tag. "Is this it, Jaime?"

"I'm not sure."

"Here, take it in your hands and examine it."

"I don't want—well, O.K."

"Is it the knife you found?"

"I think so. Except it looks cleaner now."

"Some of the bloodstains were scraped off for analysis in the police lab. Allowing for that difference, would you say this is the knife you picked up in the pumpkin field?"

"Yes, sir."

"Was it open with the blade operable the way it is now?"

"Yes, sir, open."

"Had you ever seen a knife like it before that time?"

"A couple of the boys at school carry butterfly knives."

"For show? For fun?"

"No, sir, for real."

The knife was offered in evidence, numbered, then replaced on the court clerk's table. Two of the high school students in the audience stood up to get a better view of the knife but the bailiff promptly ordered them to sit down.

"Now, Jaime," Ford said, "I want you to go over to the map on the board, and using one of the colored marking pencils, indicate the location of the pumpkin field."

"How?"

"Draw a rectangle and print the words pumpkin field beside it."

Jaime did as he was told. His hand shook and the boundaries of the pumpkin field were uneven, as though old Mr. Osborne had laid them out himself on one of his drunk days and no one had bothered to straighten them. The area where the knife was found, Jaime indicated by a circle with the letter K inside it. Then he returned to the witness box and Ford went on with the questioning.

"Jaime, I understand the pumpkin business occupied your time only for a couple of months out of the year."

"Yes, sir. Late summer and early fall."

"The rest of the year you were engaged in other projects around the ranch, is that right?"

"Yes, sir."

"Did these other jobs bring you in contact with the various crews of migrant laborers?"

"Not much. I did my work mostly after school and on weekends and holidays. Also my dad gave me orders to stay away from the mess hall and the bunkhouse."

"So you didn't become acquainted with any of the men personally?"

"No, sir. At least not very often."

"Referring now to the crew which was employed on the ranch during the first half of October, 1967, I'll ask you if any of the men were known to you by name."

"No, sir."

"Do you recall anything in particular about the crew?"

"Just the old truck they came in. It was painted dark red. I noticed that specially because it was the same color red as the pickup Felipe used to teach me to drive. It's not there any more, so I guess Mr. Osborne sold it on account of its gears being stripped too often." He added, half in contempt, half in envy, "The kids in driver education at school learn in cars with automatic shifts."

"I have no more questions, Jaime. Thank you."

Jaime went back to his place very quickly, as though he were afraid the lawyer might change his mind. But Ford's attention was already directed elsewhere, to the empty seat beside Devon.

"My witness is still missing," he told Judge Gallagher. "Robert Osborne's mother."

"Where is she?"

"I don't know."

"Well, find out."

"I'll try. I need a short recess."

"Ten minutes?"

"Half an hour would be better."

"Mr. Ford, somewhere in the county of San Diego right now, at least one irate taxpayer is figuring out exactly how much a minute this case is costing him. Do you realize that?"

"I do now, your Honor."

"Court is recessed for a period of ten minutes."

As the room began to empty, Ford walked over to where Devon was sitting. He would have liked to sit down beside her. His legs were tired and the lower part of his body felt as if the vertebrae had softened and the connecting discs had been unfastened. "Where is Mrs. Osborne?"

"She went home to rest during the noon hour but she intended to be back by one-thirty."

"I told her I was going to put her on the stand right after the lunch break. Perhaps it slipped her mind."

"I hardly think so. Mrs. Osborne is very meticulous about such things, and very punctual."

"Then perhaps one of us had better find out why she's suddenly not meticulous and punctual any more."

"Mrs. Osborne hates to be checked up on. It makes her feel old."

"It's time she got used to it," Ford said briskly. "There are pay phones at the end of the corridor."

"She might take it better if you called her."

"That's unlikely. I'm the big bad man who asks her embarrassing questions, you're her loving daughter-in-law."

"Am I?"

"Until the conclusion of this proceeding you are."

Of the half-dozen pay phones at the end of the corridor five were being used. The booths looked like upended coffins whose occupants weren't actually dead but had been put into a state of suspended animation to await a better world. The sixth booth had its door open, inviting Devon to step inside and wait too. She closed the glass door behind her, and as she'd done fifty or a hundred times in the past year, started to dial the number of Agnes Osborne's house. But her hand seemed to freeze on the dial. She couldn't remember more than the first two digits and had to look up the number in the directory as she would any stranger's. *"You're her loving daughter-in-law . . . Until the conclusion of this proceeding you are."*

The ringing of the phone was loud and sharp. She held the receiver away from her ear, so that the sound seemed a little more remote, more impersonal. Six rings, eight, ten. Agnes Osborne's house was small and she could get to the phone from any room in it, or from the patio or back yard, in less than ten rings, less than five if she hurried. And during the past year, when any call might be about Robert, she always hurried.

The booth was hot and smelled of stale tobacco and food and people. Devon opened the door a few inches, and with the little gust of new air came the sound of people talking in the alcove adjoining the row of phone booths. One of the voices was a man's, hoarse and low-pitched:

"I swear to you I didn't know a thing about it until a few minutes ago."

"Liar. You knew it all the time and wouldn't tell me. So did they. The whole bunch of you are liars."

"Listen, Carla, I'm warning you, for your own good stay away from the ranch."

"I'm not scared of the Estivars. Or the Osbornes either. My brothers see to it nobody pushes me around."

"This isn't kid stuff any more. Stay out of it."

"Look who's giving orders again like he's wearing his old cop suit and tin badge."

"Trouble, you've been nothing but trouble to me ever since I laid eyes on you."

"You laid more than eyes on me, *chicano.*"

Devon waited for another half minute, six rings, but there was no answer from Mrs. Osborne's house and no more talk from the alcove. She opened the door and stepped out into the hall.

The girl had gone. Valenzuela stood alone at the barred window of the alcove, his eyes somber and red-rimmed. When he saw Devon his mouth moved slightly as though it were shaping words he wasn't ready to speak. When he did speak, it was in a voice quite unlike the one he'd used on Carla, soft and sad, with no hint of authority in it.

"I'm sorry, Mrs. Osborne."

"What about?"

"Everything, how it's all turned out."

"Thank you."

"I wanted you to know I hoped things would be different, and the case would be solved by now. That first night when I was called out to the ranch to look for Mr. Osborne, I was sure he'd show up. Every step I took, every door I opened, every corner I went around, I expected to find him—maybe beat up a little or sick or even up to some mischief. I'm sorry things turned out this way."

"It's not your fault, Mr. Valenzuela. I'm sure you did the best you could." She wasn't sure, she'd never be sure, but it was too late now to say anything else.

"I could maybe have done better if they'd given me more money. Not more salary. Bribe money."

"*Bribe* money?"

"Don't be shocked, Mrs. Osborne. In a poor country everything's for sale, including the truth. I believe someone saw that old red truck at the border or on the road going south to Ensenada or east to Tecate; someone noticed the men in it, maybe recognized a couple of them; someone may have watched them bury the body in the desert or dump it into the sea."

"Mrs. Osborne offered a substantial reward."

"Rewards are too official, too many people are involved, too much red tape. A bribe is a nice simple family type of thing."

"Why didn't you explain the situation to me a year ago?"

"A cop can't ask a private citizen for bribe money. It wouldn't look pretty in the newspapers, it might even cause an international scandal. After all, no country likes to admit that a lot of its police, its judges, its politicians are corrupt . . . Anyway, it's over. All I'm saying now is I'm sorry, Mrs. Osborne."

"Yes. So am I."

She turned and walked toward the courtroom, holding herself rigid to counteract the feeling she had inside that vital parts had come loose and were bleeding. Someone saw the truck—noticed the men—watched them bury the body or dump it in the sea. She thought of the dozens of times she'd watched the men stooping in the fields, but they were always in the distance, always anonymous. She had wanted to get to know them a little, to be able to tell them apart, to call them by name and ask them about their homes and families, but Estivar wouldn't allow it. He said it wasn't safe, the men would misinterpret any friendliness on her part. The men, too, had obviously been given orders. When she drove past a field being harvested, they would bend low over their work, their faces hidden by the big straw hats they wore from dawn to dusk.

The light had been switched on in the sign above the door: *Quiet Please, Court Is in Session.* By the time Devon entered, the room was nearly full, the way it had been before the recess, but now the Lopez girl, as well as Mrs. Osborne, was missing.

In the aisle beside the seat Devon had occupied since the hearing began, Ford stood talking to Leo Bishop. Both men looked impatiently at Devon, as though they'd been waiting for her and had expected her to come back sooner.

Ford said, "Well?"

"There was no answer."

"Did you let it ring several minutes, in case she might be outside or in the shower or something?"

"Yes."

"Then I guess you'd better go over to the house and check up on her. Mr. Bishop here has offered to drive you or let you use his car, whichever you prefer."

"Exactly what am I supposed to do?"

"Find out if she's all right and when she intends showing up to testify."

"Why are you forcing her to testify?"

"I'm not forcing her. When I brought the subject up she seemed perfectly willing to be a witness."

"That was just a front," Devon said. "You mustn't be taken in by it."

"O.K., so I don't know her front from her back. I'm a simple man. When people tell me something I believe it, I don't immediately conclude that they mean the opposite."

"She—isn't ready to admit Robert is dead."

"She's had a whole year to get used to it. Maybe she's not trying hard enough."

"That seems a very cynical attitude."

"You'd better watch it," Ford said with a wry little smile. "You're beginning to sound like an honest-to-God loving daughter-in-law."

The door to the judge's chambers had opened and the clerk was intoning: "Remain seated and come to order. Superior Court is again in session."

"Call Ernest Valenzuela."

"Ernest Valenzuela, take the stand, please."

CHAPTER
TEN

WHEN THEY REACHED LEO'S CAR in the parking lot, he unlocked the right front door and Devon stepped inside without protest. She didn't like being dependent on Leo but she liked even less the idea of driving a car she wasn't used to in a city that was still strange to her.

Leo got in behind the wheel and turned on the ignition and the air conditioning. "I've kept away from you all day because you asked me to."

"It was Mrs. Osborne's idea," Devon said. "She thought people would talk if they saw us together."

"I'd like to think they had something to talk about . . . Do they?"

"No."

"No period, or no not yet?"

Her only response was a slight shake of her head that could have meant anything.

She had taken off the white wrist-length gloves which she'd worn almost continuously since early morning. They lay now in her lap, the false passive immaculate hands she'd exhibited to the spectators in court and strangers in the hall and on the street. Her real hands, sunburned and rough, with calloused palms and bitten nails, she showed only to friends like Leo who wouldn't care, or to people she saw every day like the Estivars and Dulzura who wouldn't notice.

"I worry about you," Leo said.

"Well, stop. I don't want you to worry about me."

"I don't want to, either, but that's the way it is. Did you have a decent lunch?"

"A hamburger."

"That's not enough. You're too thin."

"You shouldn't fuss over me, Leo."

"Why not?"

"It makes me nervous, self-conscious. I like to feel at ease with you."

"All right, no fussing. That's a promise." The humming of the air conditioner muffled the rasp in his voice.

He turned north on the freeway. Traffic had been slowed down to boulevard speed by its own volume. People passing were without names or faces or any identification except their cars: a red Mustang with Florida plates, a blue Chevelle, a VW camper decorated with daisies, a silver Continental with matching silver smoke coming from its exhaust, a yellow Dart with a black vinyl roof, a white Monaco station wagon trailing a boat. It was as if human beings existed merely to keep the vehicles in motion, and the real significance had shifted from the Smiths and the Joneses to Cougars and Corvairs, Toronados and Toyotas.

"Turn west on University," Devon said. "She lives at 3117 Ocotillo; that's three or four blocks north."

"I know where it is."

"Did Mr. Ford tell you?"

"She told me. She called me one day and asked me to come and see her."

"I thought you were barely on speaking terms."

"We barely were," Leo said. "In fact, we barely are. But I went."

"When was that?"

"About three weeks ago, as soon as she found out the hearing was scheduled for today. Well, after a lot of chitchat she finally got to the point—she wanted to make sure my wife's death wasn't brought up during the hearing. She said it was irrelevant. I agreed. She offered me a drink, which I refused, and I drove back to the ranch. That's all. At least as far as I was concerned it was all. I can't be sure what was in her mind, perhaps something quite different from what was actually said."

"Why do you suggest that?"

"If what she really wanted was to keep Ruth's name out of the proceedings, she would have called Mr. Ford, not me. I'm only a witness, he's running the show."

"Maybe she called him, too."

"Maybe." He ran his left hand around the scalloped rim of the steering wheel as though it were a bumpy road he'd never explored before. "I think she was trying to make sure I didn't say anything against her son. She had to believe—and to make other people believe—that Robert was perfect."

"What could you have said against him, Leo?"

"He wasn't perfect."

"You were referring to something specific."

"Nothing that should make any difference to you now. It was over before you even knew the Osbornes existed." He added, after a time, "It wasn't even Robert's fault. He just happened to be the boy next door. And Ruth—well, she happened to be the girl next door, only she was pushing forty and afraid of growing old."

"So the gossip about them was true."

"Yes."

"Why didn't you tell me before?"

"I started to, many times, only I never went through with it. It seemed cruel. Now—well, now I know it's necessary, cruel or not. I can't afford to let you believe Mrs. Osborne's version of Robert. He wasn't perfect. He had faults, he made mistakes. Ruth turned out to be one of the bigger mistakes but he couldn't have foreseen that. She was pretty appealing in her role of defenseless little woman, and Robert was a setup for her. He didn't even have a girl friend to stand in the way, thanks to Mrs. Osborne. She'd managed to get rid of all the girls who weren't good enough for him, and that meant all the girls. So he ended up with a married woman nearly twice his age."

Devon sat in silence, trying to imagine the two of them together, Ruth seeing in Robert another chance at youth, Robert seeing in her a chance at manhood. How often did they meet, and where? Beside the reservoir or in the grove of date palms? In the mess hall or bunkhouse when there were no migrants working on the ranch? In the ranch house itself when Mrs. Osborne went to the city? No matter where they met, people must have seen them and been shocked or amused or sympathetic—the Estivars, Dulzura, the ranch hands, perhaps even Mrs. Osborne before she shut her eyes tight and finally. Mrs. Osborne's references to Ruth had all been similar and in the same tone: "Robert was kind to the poor woman . . ." "He went out of his way to be neighborly . . ." "It was pitiful the spectacle she made of herself, but Robert was always patient and understanding."

Robert—kind, patient, understanding and neighborly. Very, very neighborly.

Devon said, "How long had it been going on?"

"I'm not sure, but I think a long time."

"Years?"

"Yes. Probably ever since he came back from school in Arizona."

"But he was just seventeen then, a boy."

"Seventeen-year-olds aren't boys. Don't waste sympathy on him. It's possible that Ruth did him a favor by distracting him from his mother."

"How can you say such a terrible thing so calmly?"

"Maybe it's not so terrible. Maybe I'm not so calm." But he sounded calm, even remote. "When Estivar was on the witness stand this morning he blamed the school for teaching Robert prejudice and keeping him away from the Estivar family. I don't believe it was prejudice. Robert simply had something new in his life, something he couldn't afford to share with the Estivars."

"If you knew about the affair, why didn't you try to stop it?"

"I did. At first Ruth denied everything. Later we had periodic fights, long and loud and no holds barred. After the last one she packed a suitcase and set out on foot for the Osbornes. She never got there."

"Then nothing was planned about her running away with Robert?"

"No. I think it would have been a real shock to him to look out and see her heading for his house with a suitcase. But he didn't see her. It had started to rain heavily and he was in the study catching up on his accounts. Mrs. Osborne was in her bedroom upstairs. Both rooms faced west, away from the river, so nobody was watching it, nobody knew the exact time of the flash flood, nobody saw Ruth try to get across. She was small and delicate like you, it wouldn't have taken much to knock her off her feet."

Small and delicate ... *"You remind me of someone back home,"* Robert had told her at their first meeting. *"Someone nice—or she used to be. She's dead now. A lot of people think I killed her."*

"Leo."

"Yes."

"Her death was an accident?"

"According to the coroner."

"And according to you?"

"To me," Leo said slowly, "it seemed a crazy way to die, drowning in the middle of a desert."

THE HOUSE AT 3117 OCOTILLO STREET was built in the California mission style, with tiled roof and thick adobe walls and an archway leading into a courtyard. The archway was decorated with ceramic tiles and from the top of it hung a miniature merry-go-round of brass horses that twitched and pranced and chimed against each other when the wind blew.

The inner court was paved with imitation flagstones and lined with shrubs and small trees growing in Mexican clay pots. The orange of the persimmon leaves, the pink of the hibiscus blossoms, the purple of the princess flowers, the crimson of the firethorn berries, all seemed lusterless and pale compared to the gaudy high-gloss paint on their containers. The word WELCOME printed on the mat outside the front door looked as though nobody had ever stepped on it. Devon's sandals sank into the thick deep velvety pile until only their tops were visible, crossed straps like two X's marking the spot: *Devon Osborne stood here.*

She pressed the door chime. Her arm felt heavy and stiff like a lead pipe attached to her shoulder.

"I don't know what to believe," she said. "I wish you hadn't told me any of it."

"Sometimes it's easy to make a hero out of a dead man, especially with the help of his mother. Well, I can't compete with heroes. If I have to cut the opposition down to size in order to win, I'll do it."

"You mustn't talk like that."

"Why not?"

"She might hear you."

"She only hears what she wants to. Anything I say isn't likely to be included."

A gust of wind blew across the courtyard. The horses on the tiny merry-go-round danced to their own music. Royal petals escaped from the princess flowers, and bamboo clawed and scratched at the living-room window.

The drapes were open and most of the room and its contents were visible. Side by side along one wall were the special possessions Mrs. Osborne had taken with her from the ranch house—the mahogany piano and the antique cherrywood desk. Both were open, as if Mrs. Osborne had played a tune and written a letter and disappeared. The rest of the furniture had come with the house, and Mrs. Osborne hadn't bothered to change any of it—a pair of flowery wing chairs facing each other across a backgammon table, a glass-fronted bookcase, and on the walls oil paintings of someone's childhood, remembered rivers, clear and sweet, emerald meadows, golden forests of maple.

Leo had walked around to the side of the house to check the garage. He returned looking irritable and worried, as though he suspected fate was about to pull another trick on him, that wheels were in motion he couldn't stop and booby traps set in places he didn't know.

"Her car's here," he said. "You'd better try the door."

"Even if it's unlocked we can't just walk in."

"Why not?"

"She wouldn't like it."

"She may not be in a position to like or dislike it."

"What does that mean?"

He didn't answer.

"Leo, are you suggesting she might have—"

"I'm suggesting we make an attempt to find out."

The knob turned easily and the door swung inward, slowed by its own weight and Devon's reluctance. As the door opened, a draught of air blew several of the papers off the desk. Leaning over to pick one up, Devon saw that it was covered with printing done with a thick-tipped black marking pen. There were sentences and half-sentences, single words, phrases, some in English, some in Spanish.

Reward   Premio   (Remuneracion? Ask Ford)
The sum of $10,000 will be paid to anyone furnishing information
(No, no. *Keep it simple.*)
On October 13, 1967
Robert K. Osborne, age 24, blond hair, blue eyes, height 6'1" weight 170
(More money?   Ask Ford)
Have you seen this man? (Use 3 pictures, front, side, ¾)
¿
¡Atencion!

Please help me find my son

Devon stood with the paper in her hand, listening to the sound of Leo moving around the dining room and the kitchen. She wondered how she could tell him that this wasn't to be the last day after all. Mrs. Osborne intended to offer another reward and the whole thing was going to start over again. There would be still another round of phone calls and letters, most of them patently ridiculous, but some reasonable enough to raise faint new hopes. The lady who claimed to have watched Robert land in a flying saucer in a field near Omaha needn't be taken seriously, yet some consideration had to be given to reports that he'd been seen working as a deckhand on a yacht anchored off Ensenada, picking up a suitcase at the TWA baggage-claim department at Los Angeles International Airport, drinking rum and Coke at a swish bar in San Francisco, running an elevator in a hotel in Denver. All reports within reason had been checked out. But Valenzuela said, "He's not working or drinking or traveling or anything else. He lost too much blood, ma'am."

Please help me find my son.

Devon put the sheet of paper back on the desk very carefully as if it were contaminated material. Then she followed Leo into the kitchen. The room had been used recently. There was a pot of coffee on the stove, the heat turned low under it, and on the work counter of the sink half a head of lettuce, two slices of bread curling a little at the edges, and an opened jar of peanut butter with a knife stuck in it. It was an ordinary table knife, blunt-tipped and dull-edged, but it may have reminded Mrs. Osborne, as it did Devon, of another more deadly knife, and she had fled the memory.

"It looks as though she started to make a sandwich," Leo said, "and something interrupted her—the doorbell maybe, or the telephone."

"She told us she was too tired to eat, that she wanted just to rest."

"Then we'd better check the bedrooms. Which is hers?"

"I don't know. She keeps changing."

The front bedroom had a window on the courtyard protected by iron grillwork and framed with bougainvillaea blossoms that fluttered in the slightest breeze like bits of scarlet tissue paper. It was fully furnished, but it had an air of abandonment about it as though the people who really belonged there had long since left the premises. The closet door was partly open and inside were half a dozen large neatly stacked cartons with Salvation Army printed in red marking pencil on each one. Devon recognized the printing as her own and the cartons as those she'd packed with Robert's stuff and given to Mrs. Osborne to deliver to the Salvation Army.

The other bedroom was occupied. Its sleeper lay face down across the bed, her body wrapped in a faded blue silk housecoat. Her arms were bent at the elbows and both hands were pressed against her head as if they were trying to protect the places where the hair was thinning. On the bureau was a Styrofoam wig stand holding the orderly curls Mrs. Osborne showed to the public. The blue hat she'd worn in court had fallen or been thrown on the carpet and her ribbon knit dress hung limply across a chair like an abandoned skin.

Both windows were shut tight. Suspended in the still air was the faint sour odor of regret, of little sins and failures mildewing in closets and damp forgotten corners.

"Mrs. Osborne," Devon said, but it sounded wrong, as if this silent helpless woman was a stranger with no right to the name.

"Mrs. Osborne, answer me. It's Devon. Are you all right?"

The stranger stirred, disclaiming the identity, protesting the invasion of her privacy when Devon leaned over and touched her temple and felt the pulse in her thin white wrist. The pulse was slow but as steady as the ticking of a clock. On the night table beside the bed there was a half-empty bottle of yellow capsules. The label identified them as Nembutal, three-quarter grain, and the prescriber as the Osbornes' family doctor in Boca de Rio.

"Do you hear me, Mrs. Osborne?"

"Go——way."

"Did you take any pills?"

"Pills."

"How many pills did you take?"

"How——? Two."

"Is that all? Just two pills?"

"Two."

"When did you take them?"

"Tired. Go away."

"Did you take them when you came home at noon?"

"Noon."

"You took two pills at noon, is that right?"

"Yes. *Yes.*"

Leo opened the windows, and the incoming air smelled of a forgotten harvest, overripe oranges whose thickened pockmarked skins covered pulp that had gone dry and fibrous. Mrs. Osborne turned over on her side, knees bent and hands over her head like a fetus trying to ward off the pain of birth.

"If she's leveling with me, she took only a hundred milligrams," Devon said. "The stuff should be wearing off pretty soon. I'll stay with her until it does."

"I'll stay too if it will help."

"It won't. She'd be upset if she woke up and found you here. You'd better go back to the courthouse and tell Mr. Ford what happened."

"I don't know what happened."

"Well, tell him as much as you do know—that she's all right but she won't be able to testify, at least not this afternoon."

CHAPTER
ELEVEN

FORD addressed the bench.

"Your Honor, the testimony of this witness, Ernest Valenzuela, has presented a number of problems. Since he is no longer employed by the sheriff's department, the files on the case are not available to him. However, I obtained permission for Mr. Valenzuela to refresh his memory by going over the files in the presence of a deputy and making notes for his appearance here today. I also arranged for a deputy to bring into the courtroom certain reports and pieces of evidence which I consider vital to this hearing."

"These reports and pieces of evidence," Gallagher said, "are they now in your possession?"

"Yes, your Honor."

"All right, proceed."

Valenzuela took the oath: the testimony he was about to give in the matter now pending before the court would be the truth and the whole truth and nothing but the truth.

Ford said, "State your name, please."

"Ernest Valenzuela."

"Where do you live, Mr. Valenzuela?"

"209 Third Street, Boca de Rio."

"Are you currently employed?"

"Yes, sir."

"Where and in what capacity?"

"I'm a salesman with the America West Insurance Company."

"How long have you held your present position?"

"Six months."

"Before that, what was the nature of your employment?"

"I was a deputy in the Boca de Rio division of the sheriff's department of San Diego County."

"For how long?"

"Since 1955 when I got out of the army, a little more than twelve years."

"Describe briefly the situation in the sheriff's department in Boca de Rio on Friday, October 13, 1967."

"The boss, Lieutenant Scotler, was on sick leave and I was in charge."

"What happened that Friday night, Mr. Valenzuela?"

"A call came in from the Osborne ranch at a quarter to eleven asking for assistance in searching for Mr. Osborne. He'd gone out earlier in the evening to look for his dog and failed to return. I picked up my partner, Larry Bismarck, at his house and we drove out to the ranch. By this time the search for Mr. Osborne had been going on for about an hour, led by Mr. Estivar, the foreman, and his son, Cruz. Mr. Osborne hadn't been located but there was considerable blood on the floor of the mess hall. I immediately phoned headquarters in San Diego and asked for reinforcements. Meanwhile my partner had found small fragments of glass on the floor of the mess hall and part of a shirt sleeve caught on a yucca spike just outside the main door. The shirt sleeve also had blood on it."

"Did you take any samples of blood?"

"No, sir. I left that to the experts."

"What did the experts do with the samples of blood they collected?"

"Sent them up to the police lab in Sacramento for analysis."

"This is the usual procedure?"

"Yes, sir."

"And at a later date you received a report of that analysis?"

"Yes, sir."

Ford turned to the bench. "Your Honor, I hereby submit a copy of the full report for you to read at your convenience. It is, naturally, detailed and technical, and in the interests of saving time—not to mention the taxpayers' money—I suggest Mr. Valenzuela be allowed to give in his own words the facts essential to this hearing."

"Granted."

"I will give Mr. Valenzuela a copy of the report also, in case his memory needs further refreshing."

Ford took two manila envelopes out of his briefcase and handed one to Valenzuela. Valenzuela accepted his reluctantly, as though he didn't need or didn't want his memory refreshed.

"The report from the police lab," Ford said, "deals with blood samples taken from four main areas—the floor of the mess hall, the piece of shirt sleeve caught on the yucca spike, the butterfly knife found by Jaime in the pumpkin field, the mouth of the dead dog. Is that correct, Mr. Valenzuela?"

"Yes, sir."

"Let's take them in the order mentioned. First, the blood on the floor of the mess hall."

"Two types were found in considerable quantity, type B positive and type AB negative. Both are uncommon types, AB negative, for example, being found in only five percent of the population."

"What about the blood found on the piece of shirt sleeve?"

"Again there were two types. The smaller amount matched some of the blood on the floor, type B, and the rest was type O. This is the commonest type, found in approximately forty-five percent of the population."

"What blood type was found on the knife?"

"AB negative."

"And in the dog's mouth?"

"Type B positive."

"Did the amount of blood found and the fact that it was of three different types lead you to any conclusions?"

"Yes, sir."

"Such as?"

"Three persons were involved in a fight. Two of them were injured seriously, the third injured to a lesser extent."

"The type O blood found on the shirt sleeve belonged to this third man?"

"Yes, sir."

From his briefcase Ford took a clear plastic bag containing a piece of blue and green plaid material. "This is the sleeve referred to?"

"Yes, sir."

"I offer it in evidence."

A few of the spectators leaned forward in their seats to

get a better look, but they soon sat back. Last year's blood appeared no more interesting than last year's coffee stains.

"Now, Mr. Valenzuela, tell us what facts were established by the contents of the plastic bag."

"The sleeve belongs to one of thousands of similar shirts sold by Sears, Roebuck through their catalog and retail stores. The shirt is a hundred percent cotton and comes in four color combinations and in sizes small, medium, large. Price in the catalog is $3.95. The style number and lot number are contained in the report of my investigation."

"In your estimation, Mr. Valenzuela, how many shirts of that style, color and size were sold by Sears Roebuck last year and the year before?"

"Thousands."

"Did you try to pinpoint the sale of that particular shirt to one particular person?"

"Yes, sir. We couldn't do it, though."

"But you were able to ascertain some facts about the man who wore the shirt, were you not?"

"Yes, sir. He was small for one thing, probably less than five foot six, 135 pounds. A number of hairs adhering to the inside of the sleeve cuff indicate that he was from one of the darker but not Negroid races."

"In view of the proximity of the Mexican border and the fact that a large percentage of the population in the area is Mexican or of Mexican descent, there is considerable likelihood that the owner of the shirt was Mexican?"

"Yes, sir."

"You didn't examine the sleeve cuff yourself, did you, Mr. Valenzuela?"

"Just superficially. The real examination was done at the police lab in Sacramento."

"Was anything significant discovered in addition to the hairs?"

"Quite a bit of dirt and oil."

"What kind of dirt?"

"Particles of sandy alkaline soil of the type found in irrigated-desert sections of the state like ours. There was a high nitrogen content in the soil, indicating the recent addition of a commercial fertilizer which is used on most ranches in the area."

"And the oil mixed with the dirt?"

"It was sebum, the secretion of human sebaceous glands. This secretion is usually abundant in younger and more active people and decreases with age."

"So a picture begins to take shape of the man who wore the shirt," Ford said. "He was small and dark, probably Mexican. He worked on one of the ranches in the area. He was young. The blood on his shirt was type O. And he got into a fight in which at least two other people were involved. Would it be possible to reconstruct this man's part in the fight?"

"I think so. The evidence seems to indicate that in the first stage of the fight he was hurt enough to bleed and that the left sleeve of his shirt was torn. He decided to escape before things got any rougher. As he ran out the door the torn sleeve caught on one of the spikes of the yucca plant and ripped completely off."

"And the other two men?"

"They finished the fight," Valenzuela said dryly.

"What can you tell us about these two men?"

"As I indicated earlier, they had different blood types, B and AB. Both of them bled considerably, especially AB."

"On the floor of the mess hall?"

"Yes, sir."

"Were samples of blood scraped off the floor and transported to the police lab in Sacramento?"

"No, sir. A section of the floor itself was removed and sent up there. This method allows a more precise analysis."

"To simplify matters I will refer to each of the three

men by their blood types. Is that agreeable to you, Mr. Valenzuela?"

"Yes, sir."

"Then O would be the dark young man who wore the green and blue plaid shirt and left the fight early after sustaining a superficial wound."

"Yes."

"Now let's turn our attention to B. What do we know about him?"

"Traces of type B blood were found in the dog's mouth."

"Robert Osborne's dog, Maxie?"

"Yes."

"Since it's highly unlikely, if not impossible, that Robert Osborne would have been attacked by his own dog, we know first of all that B was not Robert Osborne."

"There is other evidence to that effect."

"Such as?"

"Bits of human tissue, skin and hair found in the dog's mouth indicate that B was dark-skinned and dark-haired. Mr. Osborne was neither. In addition, a small shred of cloth was caught between two of the dog's teeth. The cloth was heavy-duty navy-blue cotton twill of the kind used to make men's Levis. When Mr. Osborne left the house he was wearing gray gabardine slacks. In fact, he didn't own any Levis. He wore lighter-weight, lighter-colored work clothes because of the heat in the valley."

"Getting back to the dog for a moment, when and where was it found?"

"It was found the following Monday morning, October 16, near the corner where the Osborne ranch road joins the road leading to the main highway. The exact spot is out of range of the map on the display board."

"What were the circumstances?"

"Several children from the Polk ranch, which adjoins

Mr. Bishop's, were on their way to meet the school bus when they spotted the dog's body under a creosote bush. They told the bus driver and he called us."

"Was an autopsy performed on the dog?"

"Yes, sir."

"Tell us briefly the pertinent facts."

"Multiple fractures of the skull and vertebrae indicated that the dog was struck and fatally injured by a moving vehicle such as a car."

"Or a truck."

"Or a truck."

Ford consulted his notes again. "So we had definite knowledge that the man we have called B was dark-skinned and dark-haired, that he wore Levis, that he was bitten by the dog. What else?"

"He owned, or at least used, the butterfly knife."

"How can you be sure of that?"

"The blood on the knife belonged to the other man, AB."

"Do you know who that other man was?"

"Yes, sir. Robert Osborne."

Though there was no one in the room who hadn't anticipated the answer, reaction to the spoken name seemed to be one of group surprise, simultaneous intakes of breath, sudden stirrings and rustlings and whispers.

"Mr. Valenzuela, tell the court why you're so sure the third man was Robert Osborne."

"The pieces of glass found on the mess-hall floor were identified by Dr. Paul Jarrett, an ophthalmologist, as fragments of contact lenses he had prescribed for Robert Osborne during the last week of May, 1967."

"Dr. Jarrett's report is on file as part of the record?"

"Yes, sir."

"Without going into technicalities, can you tell the court to what degree contact lenses are distinctive?"

"They're not absolutely unique the way fingerprints are, for example. But each lens has to be fitted to each eye with such precision that it's highly unlikely a mistake in identification could be made."

"Since you've brought up the subject of fingerprints, Mr. Valenzuela, let's pursue it. In reading your report of the case I was struck by the small amount of attention given to fingerprints. Will you explain this?"

"A large number of prints were lifted off the doors, walls, tables, benches, and so on. That was the trouble. Everybody and his little brother had been in and out of that mess hall." Valenzuela paused, looking guilty, as though he'd committed a punishable offense by using language not condoned by the official rule book. "There were too many fingerprints in and around the building to allow for proper classification and comparison."

"Now, Mr. Valenzuela, on November 8, nearly four weeks after Robert Osborne's disappearance, a man named John W. Pomeroy was arrested in an Imperial Beach bar. Is that correct?"

"Yes, sir."

"What was the charge?"

"Drunk and disorderly."

"Was anything pertinent to this case found among Mr. Pomeroy's effects when he was booked?"

"Yes, sir."

"What was it?"

"A credit card issued by the Pacific United Bank to Robert Osborne."

"How did it come into Mr. Pomeroy's possession?"

"He said he found it, and his story checked out. At the beginning of that week the valley had its first rain of the season. The river flooded—or, more accurately, it appeared—and a lot of debris washed down that had been accumulating for months. Pomeroy was a lifelong vagrant; searching through piles of debris was second nature to him. He picked up the credit card about a quarter of a mile downstream from the Osborne ranch."

"Is Mr. Pomeroy available for questioning in this proceeding?"

"No, sir. He died in the County Hospital of pneumonia the following spring."

"Except for the credit card found in his possession, was there anything linking him to Robert Osborne's disappearance on October 13?"

"No, sir. Pomeroy was in jail in Oakland on October 13."

"We offer in evidence exhibit number five, the credit card issued to Robert Osborne by the Pacific Union Bank ... There is one more point I'd like to bring up at this time, Mr. Valenzuela. You stated a while ago that the blood on the butterfly knife was AB negative, an uncommon type found in approximately five percent of the population. Was Robert Osborne one of this five percent?"

"Yes, sir."

"Can you offer proof of that?"

"In the summer of 1964 Mr. Osborne underwent an appendectomy. Preoperative blood tests were routinely conducted and the hospital records indicate that Robert Osborne's was AB negative."

Judge Gallagher had slumped further and further into his chair, his arms crossed over his chest giving his black robe the appearance of a strait jacket. For the most part he kept his eyes closed. The lighting in the courtroom had been cunningly engineered by experts to be too bright to look at and too dim to read by.

He said, without opening his eyes, "There is no precise law on this point, Mr. Ford, but in trying to establish the death of an absent person, it has become general practice to include an averment of diligent search."

"I was coming to that, your Honor," Ford said.

"Very well. Proceed."

"Mr. Valenzuela, did you conduct a diligent search for Robert Osborne?"

"Yes, sir."

"Indicate the time covered."

"From eleven P.M. on October 13, 1967, to the morning of April 20, 1968, when I submitted my resignation from the department."

"And the area covered?"

"By me personally, or by everyone connected with the case?"

"The whole area covered during the investigation."

"The full details are in my report. But I can summarize by saying that the search for Mr. Osborne and the search for the missing workers ultimately became the same thing. It spread out from the Osborne ranch to all the large agricultural centers of California where migrant labor is used—the Sacramento and San Joaquin and Imperial valleys, certain sections of various counties like San Luis Obispo, Santa Barbara, Ventura. Out-of-state areas included places that had served as reception centers during the bracero program, Nogales, Arizona, and El Paso, Hidalgo and Eagle Pass, Texas."

"Was there a particular part of the investigation for which you were personally responsible?"

"I checked out the names and addresses given to Mr. Estivar by the men who'd arrived at the Osborne ranch during the last week of September."

"Do you have a list of those names and addresses with you this afternoon?"

"Yes, sir."

"Would you read them aloud to the court, please?"

"Valerio Pinedo, Guaymas
Oswaldo Rojas, Saltillo
Salvador Mayo, Camargo
Victor Ontiveras, Chihuahua
Silvio Placencia, Hermosillo

131 /

Hilario Robles, Tepic
Jesus Rivera, Ciudad Juárez
Ysidro Nolina, Fresnillo
Emilio Olivas, Guadalajara
Raul Guttierez, Navojoa."

There was a brief delay while the court reporter checked with Valenzuela on the spelling of certain names. Then Ford continued: "Did anything about this list strike you as peculiar right from the beginning?"

"Yes, sir."

"Tell the court what it was."

"Well, Mexicans are very much family-oriented. It struck me as odd that no two of the men had the same name or even the same hometown. They were traveling as a unit in a single truck, yet they came from places as far apart as Ciudad Juárez and Guadalajara, nearly eighteen hundred miles. I wondered how such a mixed group had gotten together in the first place and how the truck they were driving managed to cover the distances involved. From Ciudad Juárez to the Osborne ranch, for instance, is another 750 miles. The truck was described to me by various people as an ancient G.M., and on the stand this morning Mr. Estivar said it was burning so much oil it looked like a smokestack."

"Did you, on seeing the list, immediately sense that something was wrong?"

"Yes, sir. Normally a group of ten men like that would come from just two or three families, all living in the same area and probably not far from the border."

"So when you started into Mexico to try and find the missing men, you already suspected that the names and addresses they'd given Mr. Estivar were fictitious and their papers forged?"

"Yes, sir."

"Did you, in spite of this, conduct a diligent search of all the areas?"

"I did."

"And you found no trace of Robert Osborne or of the men who'd been employed at the Osborne ranch?"

"None."

"During this time other police departments in the Southwest joined the search and bulletins were circulated throughout the country."

"Yes, sir."

"At the end of November, Robert Osborne's mother offered a $10,000 reward for information about her son, dead or alive."

"You know more about that than I do, Mr. Ford."

Ford made a quarter-turn to face the bench. "Your Honor, this reward was handled through my office at Mrs. Osborne's request. Notices of it were posted in public buildings, and ads were placed, in two languages, in newspapers both in this country and Mexico. There was also considerable news coverage on radio and TV, mainly in the Tijuana–San Diego area. I rented a P.O. box to receive mail and a special phone was installed in my office for calls. The reward generated plenty of interest—$10,000 usually does. We had a lot of crank calls and letters, a couple of false confessions, anonymous tips, astrological readings, suggestions on how the money might better be spent and a few assorted threats. One woman even appeared at my office carrying a crystal ball in a bowling bag. No useful information was received from the crystal ball or any other source, so on my advice Mrs. Osborne withdrew the offer and all ads and notices were canceled."

The judge opened his eyes and gave Valenzuela a brief penetrating glance. "As I understand it, Mr. Valenzuela, from October 13, when Robert Osborne disappeared, until April 20, when you resigned from the sheriff's office, your full time was spent in trying to locate Robert Osborne and/or the men allegedly responsible for his disappearance."

"Yes, your Honor."

"That would seem to constitute a diligent search on your part."

"Many others were involved. Some still are. A case like this is never officially closed even though the deputies are assigned to other jobs."

"I believe it's legitimate for me to ask whether your resignation from the sheriff's department was due in part to your failure to locate Mr. Osborne and the missing men."

"It wasn't, your Honor. I had personal reasons." Valenzuela rubbed one side of his jaw as though it had begun to hurt. "Nobody likes to fail, naturally. If I'd found what I was looking for, I would have hesitated before going into another line of work."

"Thank you, Mr. Valenzuela." Judge Gallagher leaned back in his chair and recrossed his arms on his chest. "You may continue, Mr. Ford."

"Has diligent search been proved to your Honor's satisfaction?"

"Of course, of course."

"Now, Mr. Valenzuela, during the six months you worked on the case you must have reached some conclusions about what happened to the ten missing men."

"There is no doubt in my mind that they crossed the border, probably before they were even missed at the ranch and before the police knew a crime had been committed. The men had a truck and they had papers. Once they were back in their own country they were safe."

"How safe?"

"Let's put it in terms of figures," Valenzuela said. "At that time Tijuana had a population exceeding 200,000 and a police force with only eighteen squad cars."

"All vehicles are stopped at the border, aren't they?"

"The Tijuana–San Diego border is said to be the busiest in the world, 20,000,000 people a year. This averages out to 54,000 a day, but in actual fact weekday traffic is much lighter and weekend traffic much heavier. Between a Friday afternoon and a Sunday night 300,000 people or more travel between the two countries. Numbers alone present a very serious problem to law enforcement agencies. There are also other factors. Mexican laws differ from U.S. laws, enforcement in many areas is inconsistent, bribery of officials is a general practice, policemen are few and usually poorly trained."

"How much chance did you figure you had of locating the missing men once they'd crossed the border into their own country?"

"When I started out I thought there was some chance. As time went on, it became obvious there wasn't any. The reasons have been mentioned—generalized corruption, overcrowding and understaffing at the border, lack of training, discipline and morale among Mexican police officers. Such statements aren't going to make me very popular among certain people, but facts must be faced. I'm not inventing anything in order to justify my own failure in this case."

"Your candor is appreciated, Mr. Valenzuela."

"Not by everybody."

Valenzuela's smile appeared and disappeared so fast that Ford wasn't quite sure he'd seen it and not at all sure it had been a smile. Perhaps it was merely a grimace indicating a twinge of pain in the head or stomach or conscience.

"One more item of interest, Mr. Valenzuela. There's been considerable talk about the blood found on the floor of the mess hall. Between the mess hall and the bunkhouse there's an area of blacktop. Was any blood found on it?"

"No, sir."

"Near it?"

"No, sir."

"What about the bunkhouse?"

"It was a mess, as the photographs in the file clearly indicate, but there were no bloodstains."

"Was it possible to determine if anything had been taken from the bunkhouse?"

"Not that night. The following day a careful examination was made with Mr. Estivar present and it was discovered that three blankets were missing from one of the bunks, a striped flannelette, more like a double sheet, and two brown wool, army surplus."

"Did you connect the fact that no bloodstains were found outside the mess hall with the fact that three blankets were missing from the bunkhouse?"

"Yes, sir. It seemed reasonable to assume that Mr. Osborne's body had been wrapped in the blankets before it was removed from the mess hall."

"Why three blankets? Why not two? Or one?"

"One or two probably wouldn't have been adequate," Valenzuela said. "A young man of Mr. Osborne's height and weight carries between six and a half and seven quarts of blood in his system. Even if as much as two quarts were found on the floor of the mess hall, there would have been enough left to cause a lot of trouble for the other men."

"You mean the other two men who were involved in the fight?"

"Yes, sir—O, who left the fight early, and B, who lost a considerable amount of blood."

"Your previous evidence indicated that both of these men were small."

"Yes, sir."

"Did you know Robert Osborne personally, Mr. Valenzuela?"

"Yes, sir."

"How would you describe his physique?"

"He was tall, not heavy but well-muscled and strong."

"Could two small men, both wounded, one of them

quite badly, have been able to wrap Mr. Osborne's body in blankets and carry it out to a vehicle?"

"I can't give you a definite answer to that. Under special circumstances people can sometimes do things which ordinarily would be impossible for them."

"Since you can't give a definite answer, perhaps you will tell the court your opinion."

"My opinion is that O, the man who was wounded slightly, went to get help from his friends."

"And got it?"

"And got it."

"Mr. Valenzuela, in California jurisprudence it is held that where absence from any cause other than death is inconsistent with the nature of the person absent, and the facts point to the reasonable conclusion that death has occurred, the court is justified in finding death as a fact. However, if the person at the time he was last seen was a fugitive from justice or was a bankrupt, or if from other causes it would be improbable that he would be heard from even if alive, then no inference of death will be drawn. That's perfectly clear, is it not?"

"Yes, sir."

"Now as Mr. Osborne's lawyer I can testify he was not a bankrupt. Was he a fugitive from justice, Mr. Valenzuela?"

"No, sir."

"Was there, to your knowledge, any other cause, or causes, which would prevent Mr. Osborne from getting in touch with his relatives and friends?"

"Not to my knowledge, no."

"Can you think of any reason at all why an inference of death should not be drawn?"

"No, sir."

"Thank you, Mr. Valenzuela. I have no more questions."

As Valenzuela left the stand the court clerk rose to

announce the usual afternoon recess of fifteen minutes. Ford asked that it be extended by half an hour to let him prepare his summary, and after some discussion the extra time was granted.

The bailiff once again opened the doors. He was getting bored and weary. Dead people took up a great deal of his time.

CHAPTER
TWELVE

LIKE AN ANIMAL that had sensed danger in its sleep, Mrs. Osborne awakened abruptly and completely. Her opening eyes were alert, ready to spot an enemy, her voice distinct, ready to challenge one: "What are you doing here?"

"You didn't answer your phone," Devon said, turning from the window. "I came out to see why. The front door was unlocked, so I walked in."

"To check up on me."

"Yes."

"As if I were some doddering old fool."

"No. Mr. Ford suggested I find out why you didn't return to court this afternoon. He thought he'd made it clear that you were expected to testify."

"He made it quite clear." Mrs. Osborne sat up on the bed, running her fingers along her chin and cheeks and forehead like a blind woman reacquainting herself with her own face. "I don't always do what's expected of me, especially when I think it's wrong. I couldn't stop the hearing but at least I could keep from playing a part in it."

"And you feel that's a victory?"

"It was the best I could do at the moment."

"At the moment," Devon repeated. "Then you have something else in mind?"

"Yes."

"Such as a new reward?"

"So you saw the paper on my desk. Well, I was going to tell you anyway." She stood up, holding the collar of the blue robe tight against her throat as if to protect a vulnerable place. "Naturally you disapprove. But it's too late. I've already arranged for the first ad in the paper."

"It seems like a useless gesture."

"Ten thousand dollars is more than a gesture. It's a good solid chunk of reality."

"Only if it buys something," Devon said. "And there's nothing to buy. The other reward didn't bring in a single usable piece of information."

"This second one will be different. For instance, I'm going to arrange for a much wider distribution of reward posters. And the posters themselves will be redesigned. This time we'll use at least two pictures of Robert, full face and profile—you can help me choose—and the wording will be kept very simple and direct so that the meaning will get across even in the smaller Mexican villages where hardly anyone is literate." She let out a sudden little laugh, almost like a schoolgirl's giggle. "Why, I feel better already just talking about it. It always cheers me up to take positive action on my own instead of waiting for other people to make the decisions. I'll put on a fresh pot of coffee to celebrate. You'll have some, won't you, dear?"

She left the room without waiting for an answer, and after a brief hesitation Devon followed her out into the kitchen. Mrs. Osborne poured water into the percolator and measured the coffee with a plastic scoop, humming to herself in a loud nervous monotone intended to cover up awkward silences, discourage awkward questions. It was like the piano playing Estivar had told Devon about during the noon recess: *"She'd start playing to cover up, a piece with good firm chords like 'March of the Toreadors' . . . 'Onward, Christian Soldiers' . . . Bang bang bang . . . Sometimes I swear I can hear the sound of that piano, though it isn't even there any more, I helped the movers take it out of the house myself."*

Suddenly the humming stopped and Mrs. Osborne turned, frowning, from the window. "I don't see your car in the driveway. How did you get here?"

"Leo brought me."

"Oh."

"He had no trouble finding the place," Devon said in a careful voice. "Apparently he'd been here before."

"I sent for him two or three weeks ago to discuss a personal matter."

"Ruth."

"He told you, then."

"Yes."

Mrs. Osborne sat down at the table across from Devon, one corner of her mouth hooked in an iron smile. "He probably repeated that ugly story about Ruth and Robert."

"Yes."

"Of course you didn't believe it. Why, Robert could have had dozens of girls, young, pretty, rich. It's unthinkable that he'd have bothered with a woman like Ruth who had nothing. It simply doesn't make sense, does it?"

Devon said, "No," because it was expected of her. She no longer knew what to believe, what made sense and what didn't. Each new piece of information cast a shadow instead of a light; Robert was gradually disappearing into darkness, and the months they had spent together were losing their outlines, changing shape like clouds on a stormy day.

The coffee had begun to percolate and for a time its cheerful bubbling was the only sound in the room.

Then Mrs. Osborne spoke again: "After she died, the gossips had a field day, of course. The funny thing was, they didn't blame Leo for neglecting his wife, or Ruth for seeking the company of another man. They blamed Robert."

"Why?"

"Because he was young and vulnerable."

"That's not reason enough."

"His very existence was reason enough for some people. Wherever Robert and I went, we stepped into the midst of whispers. The phone would ring and there'd be no one on the line, just the sound of breathing. Letters arrived, unsigned. I finally called the sheriff's office and they sent Valenzuela out to the ranch to discuss the situation. Well, we talked but there was no communication. He was carrying around in his mind a picture of Robert as the neighborhood seducer and destroyer of women, and I couldn't shake it loose. He's been prejudiced against Robert right from the beginning, that's why he never really tried to find him. He didn't want to. Oh, he put on a good show, taking all those trips to the labor camps and into Mexico. It fooled his superiors for a while but they caught on eventually and fired him."

"I heard that he quit because he got married again and his new wife didn't like him being in police work."

"Nonsense. He'd never have given up the power of

such a job, let alone his seniority and his pension, for the sake of some little tramp."

"How do you know she was a little tramp? She might—"

"Word gets around. Valenzuela was fired. I heard it on the valley grapevine as well as the Mexicans' *parra grande.*"

"I talked to him this afternoon," Devon said. "He apologized for the way things have turned out. He seemed very sincere. I can't believe he didn't do his best to find Robert."

"Can't you . . . ? How do you take your coffee?"

"Black, please."

"I'm afraid it's rather weak."

"That's all right."

Mrs. Osborne poured the coffee, her hand steady. "What else did he have to say? Surely he didn't just walk up to you and tell you he was sorry."

"He said the case is over."

"As far as he's concerned it's been over for a long time."

"No. He meant that I—you and I—shouldn't go on hoping."

"Well, his advice was wasted on both of us, wasn't it? You never really started hoping, and I don't intend to stop."

"I know that," Devon said. "I saw the cartons."

"Cartons?"

"In the bedroom closet. The ones you told me you were going to take to the Salvation Army."

"I made no promise. I agreed to take them because I didn't want to argue with you. You were so anxious to get them out of the house. It seemed the natural move to make, bringing them here instead of giving them away to strangers. Some of the things in the cartons were very personal. His glasses." Her voice tripped over the word, fell, rose again. "How could you do that, Devon—give away his *glasses?*"

"They might help someone to see. Robert would have approved."

"It saddened me terribly to think of a stranger wearing Robert's glasses, perhaps using them to see ugliness Robert would never have seen because he was such a good boy. No, I couldn't bear it. I put his glasses away for safekeeping."

"What are you going to do with the rest of his stuff?"

"I thought I'd fix up the front bedroom, just the way his room was at the ranch, with the kind of things boys like— college pennants on the walls, and surfing posters and, of course, the maps. Did Robert ever show you his old maps?"

"No."

"My sister sent them to him for his birthday one year. They were framed copies of early medieval maps showing the world as it was presumed to be then, flat and sur- rounded by water. At the edge of one map there was a notice saying that further areas were unknown and unin- habitable because of the sun's heat. Another said simply, 'Beyond this point are monsters.' The phrase appealed to Robert. He printed a sign and taped it outside his door: BEYOND THIS POINT ARE MONSTERS. Dulzura hated the sign and wouldn't go past it because she believed in monsters, probably still does. She refused to clean Rob- ert's room unless I stood in the doorway to protect her, just in case. Dulzura's lucky. The rest of us have monsters too, but we must call them by other names, or pretend they don't exist . . . The world of Robert's maps was nice and flat and simple. It had areas for people and areas for monsters. What a shock it is to discover the world is round and the areas merge and nothing separates the monsters and ourselves; that we are all whirling around in space together and there isn't even a graceful way of falling off. Knowledge can be a dreadful thing."

Devon sipped the coffee. It was like hot water, slightly colored, barely scented. "How old was Robert when he was given the maps?"

"I'm not sure."

"Jaime's age?"

"A little more than that, I think."

"Fifteen, then."

"Yes, I remember now, it was the year he grew. He'd been rather small until then, not much taller than the Estivar boys, and he suddenly started to grow."

He was fifteen, Devon thought. *It was the year of his father's death and she sent him away to school. He never really came back. She's still waiting for his return to a room decorated with school pennants and surfing posters and a warning sign on the door.*

CHAPTER
THIRTEEN

FOR THE LAST TIME that day the bailiff announced that court was in session, and Ford addressed the bench:

"Your Honor, I would like at this time to summarize the events which led to the filing of the petition by Devon Suellen Osborne alleging that her husband, Robert Kirkpatrick Osborne, met his death on the night of October 13, 1967, and asking the court to declare him officially dead and to appoint her as administrator of his estate. Nine witnesses have been heard. Their testimony has given us a fairly complete picture of Robert Osborne.

"Robert Osborne was a young man of twenty-four, happily married, in good health and spirits, and planning for the future, both the very near future—he was driving into San Diego that morning to pick up a new tennis racket, attend a growers' luncheon, visit his mother, and so on— and the distant future—his wife was expecting a child. He was the sole owner of a ranch. It would never have made him a millionaire but it was operating in the black and he had only himself and his wife to support, his mother having inherited money from her sister. The troubles in his life were minor, mainly concerned with the management of the ranch, the difficulty of getting adequate help at harvest time, and so on.

"On the morning of October 13, 1967, Robert Osborne rose, as usual, before dawn, showered and dressed. He wore gray lightweight gabardine slacks and a dacron jacket in a gray and black plaid pattern. He kissed his wife goodbye, asked her to be on the lookout for his dog, Maxie, who'd been gone all night, and told her he'd be home for dinner about seven-thirty that evening. Acting on doctor's orders, Mrs. Osborne remained in bed. Before she went back to sleep she heard her husband outside calling the dog.

"Mr. Secundo Estivar, the next witness, testified that Robert Osborne appeared at his door while the family was having breakfast. He had the dog with him and acted very upset because he thought it had been poisoned. There was an exchange of angry words between the two men, then Robert Osborne departed, carrying the dog in his arms. It was still early when he appeared at the veterinary hospital run by Dr. John Loomis. He left the dog at the hospital for diagnosis and continued on his way to San Diego. As he drove toward the highway he saw Carla Lopez walking along the street and stopped to ask her about the possibility of her two older brothers coming back to work for him.

He told Miss Lopez his present crew was no good and had no experience.

"The crew he referred to was composed of ten *viseros*, Mexican nationals with visas which allowed them to do agricultural work in the United States. Mr. Estivar made a record of the names and addresses of the men but he didn't examine their visas carefully nor did he check the registration of the truck they arrived in. Such things seemed unimportant at the time. The tomato crop was ready to be picked and crated and the need for pickers was aggravated by other factors. During the preceding month one of Mr. Estivar's sons, Rufo, had married and moved to Northern California; another, Felipe, had left to look for a non-agricultural job, and the border-crossers who'd been working the fields had their minibus stolen in Tijuana and were without transportation. It was a critical period at the ranch, with Mr. Estivar and his oldest son, Cruz, putting in sixteen-hour days to keep things going. When the ten *viseros* showed up, they were hired on the spot, no questions asked.

"They remained for two weeks. During those two weeks they kept, and were kept, to themselves. As Mr. Estivar remarked from the witness box, he was not running a social club. The bunkhouse where the *viseros* slept, the mess hall where they ate their meals were out of bounds for Mrs. Estivar and Jaime and his younger sisters, for Mrs. Osborne, for the cook, Dulzura Gonzales, and even the Osborne dog. This isolation made the job of the sheriff's department not only difficult but, as it turned out, impossible. The men Mr. Valenzuela spent six months searching for were hardly more than shadows. They left no tracks and no pictures in anyone's memory, no gaps in anyone's life. Their main identity was an old red G.M. truck.

"The truck departed from the ranch late in the afternoon of October 13. Around nine o'clock that night, as Mr. Estivar was preparing for bed, he heard the truck return.

149 /

He recognized it by the peculiar squeak of its brakes and the fact that it parked outside the bunkhouse. The Estivar family kept ranchers' hours. Shortly after nine they were asleep, Mr. and Mrs. Estivar, the two sons who were still living at home, Cruz, the oldest, and Jaime, the youngest, and the nine-year-old twin girls. We have reason to believe they all slept through a murder.

"The victim, Robert Osborne, had arrived home about seven-thirty from his trip to the city. He had his dog with him, completely recovered and eager to run after being cooped up at the vet's all day. He let it out and proceeded into the house, where he had dinner with his wife. According to her it was a pleasant meal lasting an hour or so. At approximately eight-thirty Robert Osborne went into the kitchen to give Dulzura Gonzales some money for her birthday, since he'd forgotten to buy her a present in San Diego. He took a twenty-dollar bill out of his wallet. Miss Gonzales noticed that the wallet contained a lot of money. We don't know the actual amount, but it hardly matters—murders have been committed for twenty-five cents. What matters is that when Robert Osborne left the house he had in his possession enough money to constitute what Miss Gonzales called 'a real temptation to a poor man.'

"While Robert Osborne was outside looking for the dog, his wife, Devon, went into the main living room to play an album of symphonic music which had recently arrived by mail. It was a warm night after a hot day and the windows were still closed. The drapes had been opened after sunset, but the windows faced east and south toward the riverbed, the Bishop ranch and the city of Tijuana. Only the city was visible. Devon Osborne did some straightening up around the room while she listened to the music and waited for her husband's return. Time passed, too much time. She began to worry in spite of the fact that Robert Osborne had been born on the ranch and knew every inch of it. Finally she went out to the garage, thinking that her husband might have driven to one of the neighboring ranches. His car was still there. She then telephoned Mr. Estivar.

"It was almost ten o'clock and the Estivar family was asleep, but Mrs. Osborne let the phone ring until Mr. Estivar answered. When he learned of the situation he asked Mrs. Osborne to stay inside the house with the doors and windows locked while he and his son, Cruz, searched for Robert Osborne with a jeep. Following instructions Mrs. Osborne waited in the kitchen. At a quarter to eleven Mr. Estivar came back to the ranch house to call the sheriff's office in Boca de Rio. Mr. Valenzuela, with his partner, Mr. Bismarck, arrived at the ranch within half an hour. They discovered a great deal of blood on the floor of the mess hall and called the main office in San Diego for reinforcements.

"More blood was found later that night on a piece of cloth caught on a yucca spike outside the mess-hall door. The cloth was part of a sleeve from a man's shirt, small in size. On the following Monday children waiting for a school bus came across the body of Robert Osborne's dog, which an autopsy later showed had been struck by a car or truck. About three weeks later, on November 4, Jaime Estivar spotted the butterfly knife among the pumpkin vines. The floor of the mess hall, the sleeve, the dog's mouth and the butterfly knife—these were the main areas where blood was found and from which samples were sent to the police lab in Sacramento for analysis. Three types of blood were classified, B, AB and O. Type O was confined to the sleeve; both B and AB were in considerable quantity on the floor; B was in the dog's mouth and AB on the butterfly knife.

"Additional clues turned up in the lab. Tiny fragments of glass from the mess-hall floor were identified as the contact lenses Robert Osborne was wearing when he left the house. The torn sleeve contained particles of sandy alkaline soil with a high nitrogen content indicating recent use of a commercial fertilizer. Such soil is typical of the Valley area. Mixed with the sample taken from the sleeve was sebum, the secretion of human oil glands which flows more copiously in young people, and a number of straight black hairs belonging to someone from one of the dark but not Negroid races. Similar hairs and bits of human tissue were found in the dog's mouth, as well as a shred of cloth, heavy-duty blue cotton twill of the kind used to make men's work pants.

"From a police lab five hundred miles away, a picture began to emerge of the events which took place on the Osborne ranch that night and of the men who participated in them. There were three. The only one whose name we know was Robert Osborne. Let us refer to the other two, as we did previously, by their blood types. Type O was a dark-haired, dark-skinned young man, small in stature, probably Mexican, who worked on a ranch in the area. He wore a blue and green plaid cotton shirt of the kind sold by the thousands through Sears Roebuck. He was slightly wounded near the beginning of the fight and left early, catching his sleeve on a yucca spike as he ran out the door. Perhaps O was merely trying to escape further trouble, but it seems more likely that he went to get help for his friend, seeing that things were going badly. The friend, B, was also dark-skinned, dark-haired and probably Mexican. He wore Levis and carried a butterfly knife. Lum Wing referred to such a knife as 'jewelry,' but it was lethal jewelry. A butterfly knife in the right hands can be almost as quick and deadly as a switchblade. We know that B was bitten by the dog and also that he was fairly seriously injured in the fight.

"I will not attempt to reconstruct the crime itself, how and why it started, whether it was actually planned as a robbery or a murder, or whether it was a chance encounter that turned into a homicide. We simply don't know. The lab that tells us a man's age, race, stature, blood type, clothing can't reveal what's going on inside his head. Our only clue concerning events prior to the crime was provided by Lum Wing, the cook, whose quarters were in a partitioned-off area at one end of the mess hall. Mr. Wing testified that he dozed off on his cot after drinking some wine. He was awakened by the sound of loud angry voices talking in Spanish. He didn't recognize the voices or understand what they were saying, since he doesn't speak the language. Nor did he attempt to interfere in the argument. He made earplugs out of small pieces of paper, put them in his ears and went back to sleep.

"While the circumstances leading up to the crime itself are and will probably remain obscure, what happened afterward is somewhat clearer. First, there is the evidence of the blankets missing from the bunkhouse—a double flannelette sheet-type blanket and two brown wool army surplus—plus the fact that no bloodstains were found outside the mess hall. Mr. Valenzuela has testified that the body of a young man Robert Osborne's size contains between six and a half and seven quarts of blood. It's a reasonable assumption that the body was wrapped in the three blankets and carried out to the old red G.M. truck. Ten men had arrived in that truck. Eleven left in it.

"As the vehicle moved toward the main road three things occurred: the murder weapon was tossed out into the pumpkin field; the dog was struck and killed as it chased the truck in pursuit of its master; and some of the contents of Robert Osborne's wallet, if not the wallet itself, were thrown into the riverbed. One item, a credit card, was subsequently found downstream in a pile of debris after the season's first heavy rain. Unlike other cards Robert Osborne carried in his wallet, the credit card was made of a heavy plastic, indestructible in water. If the men had been ordinary robbers they'd probably have kept the card and tried to use it. But the chances are that the *viseros* didn't even know what it was, let alone that it could be useful to them.

"In hearings like this one, as your Honor pointed out, an averment of diligent search should be included. The search was diligent, indeed. It began the night Robert Osborne disappeared and has continued until the present time, a period of one year and four days. It covered an area from Northern California to Eastern Texas, from Tijuana to Guadalajara. It included the posting, by the victim's mother, of a ten-thousand-dollar reward, none of which was ever paid out because no legitimate claim was filed.

"When a man drops out of sight, leaving behind evidence of foul play but no body, questions inevitably arise in people's minds. Was the disappearance voluntary and the evidence faked? Would a presumption of death benefit the man or his survivors? Was he in trouble with the law, with his family, his friends? Was he depressed? Ill? Broke? In the case of Robert Osborne such questions are easily answered. He was a young man with everything to live for. He had a loving wife, a devoted mother, a child on the way, a successful ranch, good health, good friends.

"I will let Devon Osborne's own words conclude this summary. She said in her testimony this morning: 'I was sure my husband was dead. I'd been sure for a long time. Nothing would keep Robert from getting in touch with me if he were alive!' "

CHAPTER
FOURTEEN

ON THE WAY HOME LUM WING, exhausted by his mental battles with the law and his unexpected victory, fell asleep in the back of the station wagon.

The day had had the opposite effect on Jaime. He felt excited and restless. Splashes of bright red crossed his face, disappeared and came back again like warning lights turning on and off. Around his family and friends he was used to playing it cool, limiting his reactions to blank stares, noncommittal shrugs or barely perceptible movements of the head. Now suddenly he wanted to talk, talk a great deal, to anyone. Only Dulzura was available, massive and quiet in the seat beside him. All the talking was being done in the front seat. It wasn't loud, it didn't sound like quarreling, and yet Jaime knew it was and listened to find out why.

"... Judge Gallagher, not Galloper."

"Very well. Gallagher. How did he get to be a judge if he can't make up his mind?"

"He can," Estivar said. "He probably already has."

"Then why didn't he announce it?"

"That's not the way it's done. He's supposed to go over all the testimony and study the reports from the police lab before he reaches a decision."

When Ysobel was angry her speech became very precise. "It seems to me the lawyer was attempting to prove the *viseros* killed Mr. Osborne. Accusing men who are not present to defend themselves is not American justice."

"They weren't present because they couldn't be found. If they'd been found they would have had a fair trial."

"Men do not just disappear into the air like smoke."

"Some do. Some did."

"Still, it doesn't seem rightful to read names out loud and in court the way they did. Supposing one of the names had been yours and you weren't given a chance to say, 'That's me, Secundo Estivar, that's my name, don't you go accusing—' "

"The names read in court were not real, can't you understand that?"

"Even so."

"All right. If you don't like the way Mr. Ford handled the case, call him up and tell him as soon as we get home. But don't drag me in."

"You are in," Ysobel said. "You gave him the names."

"I had to, I was ordered to."

"Even so."

It was a dangerous subject, this business of the migrants, and Estivar knew his wife wouldn't give it up until she was offered another to take its place. He said, "You'd have handled the case much better than Ford did, of course."

"In some ways maybe I could."

"Well, keep a list and send it to him. Don't waste time telling me. I'm no—"

"I don't think he should have brought the girl into it, Carla Lopez." Ysobel rubbed her eyes as though she were erasing an image. "It was a shock to me seeing her again. I thought she'd left town, and good riddance. Then suddenly up she pops, in court of all places, and no longer a girl. A woman, a woman with a baby. I suppose you saw the baby when she had it with her this morning."

"Yes."

"Do you think it looked like—"

"It looked like a baby," Estivar said stonily. "Any baby."

"What fools we were to hire her that summer."

"I didn't hire her. You did."

"It was your idea to get someone who'd be good with the kids."

"Well, she was good with the kids, all right, only it was the big kids, not the little ones."

"How was I to foresee that? She looked so innocent," Ysobel said. "So pure. I never dreamed she'd dangle herself in front of my sons like a—like a—"

"Lower your voice."

Jaime leaned toward Dulzura and spoke in a whisper: "What's that mean, dangled herself?"

Dulzura wasn't certain but she had no intention of admitting it to a fourteen-year-old boy. "You're too young to know such things."

"Bull."

"You get fresh with me and I'll tell your father. He'll knock the bejeez out of you."

"Oh, come on. What's it mean, she dangled herself?"

"It means," Dulzura said carefully, "that she paraded around with her chest stuck out."

"Like a drum majorette?"

"Yes. Only no music or drums. No costume or baton, either."

"Then what's left?"

"The chest."

"What's so great about that?"

"I told you, you're too young."

Jaime studied the row of warts along the knuckles of his left hand. "Her and Felipe used to meet in the packing shed."

"Well, don't you tell nobody. It's none of their business."

"There are cracks between the boards where I could watch them through."

"You oughta be ashamed."

"She didn't dangle herself," Jaime said. "She just took off her clothes."

THE FIVE O'CLOCK RACE to the suburbs had begun and cars were spilling wildly onto the freeway from every ramp. With the windows open, the way Leo liked to drive, conversation was impossible. Above the din of traffic, only very loud noises could have been audible, shouts of anger, excitement, fear. Devon felt only a kind of gray and quiet grief. The tears that stung her eyes dried in the wind and left a dusting of salt across her lashes. She made no attempt to wipe it away.

Leo took the off-ramp to Boca de Rio and it was then that the first words of the journey were exchanged.

"Would you like to stop for a cup of coffee, Devon?"

"If you would."

"It's up to you. You're a free agent now, remember? You have to start making decisions."

"All right. I'd like some coffee."

"See how easy it is?"

"I guess so." She didn't tell him that her decision had nothing to do with coffee or with him. She only wanted to make sure she wouldn't be returning to an empty house, that Dulzura would have plenty of time to get home before she did.

They stopped at a small roadside *cantina* on the outskirts of Boca de Rio. The proprietor, after a voluble exchange of greetings with Leo in Spanish, led the way to a table beside the window. It was a picture window without much of a picture, a stunted paloverde tree and a patch of weeds half-dead of drought.

She said, as though there'd been no lapse of time since midafternoon and the ride to Mrs. Osborne's house, "Robert must have had some girl friends."

"Temporary ones. None of them hung around after a few bouts with Mrs. Osborne."

"Robert wasn't a weak or timid man. Why didn't he stand up to her?"

"She was pretty subtle about it, I guess. Maybe he didn't realize what was going on. Or maybe he didn't care."

"You mean he had no need of anyone besides Ruth." She stared out at the patch of weeds dying hard like hope. "Leo, listen. There's no—no reasonable doubt that he and Ruth—"

"No reasonable doubt."

"All those years, ever since he was a boy?"

"I repeat, seventeen-year-olds aren't boys. Some fifteen-year-olds aren't either."

"What are you hinting at?"

"He was fifteen when she sent him away to school."

"But that was because his father died."

"Was it? The usual pattern in such cases is for the mother to lean more heavily on the son, not send him away."

The proprietor brought mugs of coffee and a dish containing slivers of dark sweet Mexican chocolate to sprinkle on top. The chocolate melted as soon as it touched the hot liquid, leaving tiny fragrant pools of oil which caught the sun and shone iridescent like little round rainbows.

Leo broke up the rainbows with the tip of a spoon. "I've been thinking a lot lately about those two years he was gone, remembering things, some trivial, some important. Ruth was depressed—I remember that well enough. It colored our lives. She told me that every hour was like a big blob of gray she couldn't see through or over or underneath."

"What about Mrs. Osborne?"

"She kept pretty much to herself—normal enough for a woman who'd just lost her husband. The Osbornes had very little social life because of Osborne's drinking, so Mrs. Osborne's seclusion wasn't particularly noticeable. We'd never seen much of her anyway, now we saw less." The miniature rainbows in his cup had re-formed and he broke them up again. "I recall one occasion when I asked Ruth to go over and visit Mrs. Osborne, thinking it might do them both some good. Ruth surprised me by agreeing right away. In fact, she even baked a cake to take with her. She started out on foot toward the Osborne ranch—she couldn't drive a car and she turned down my offer of a ride. She stayed away for hours. She was still gone when I finished work for the day, so I went to look for her. I found her sitting on the edge of the dry riverbed. There was a flock of blackbirds beside her and she was feeding the cake to them piece by piece. She looked quite happy. I hadn't seen her look that happy for a long time. Without saying a word she got in the car and we drove home. She never told me what happened, I never asked. That was nine years ago, yet it's one of the most vivid pictures I have left of Ruth, her sitting quietly on the riverbank feeding cake to a bunch of blackbirds."

"She liked to feed things?"

"Yes. Dogs, cats, birds, anything that came along."

"So did Robert." She looked out at the falling sun. "Perhaps they were just good friends, just very good friends."

"Perhaps."

"I'd like to go home now, Leo."

"All right."

THE PUNGENT SMELL of oregano drifting out of the kitchen windows welcomed her home.

Dulzura was at the work counter shredding cheese for enchiladas. She said, without turning, "Are you O.K.?"

"Yes. Thank you."

"I thought, an early dinner with a little wine— How about that?"

"Fine."

"Did I do right in court? I was nervous, maybe people couldn't hear me."

"They heard you."

"What kind of wine would you like?"

Devon was on the point of saying "Any kind," when she remembered Leo's insisting that she start making decisions on her own. "Port."

"All we got is sherry. The only reason I asked is because you always say you don't care what kind."

So much for decisions, Devon thought, and went upstairs to take a shower.

After dinner Devon walked by herself in the warm still night. The sound of her footsteps, inaudible to a human being, was picked up by a barn owl. He hissed a warning to his mate, who was hunting for rats outside the packing shed and underneath the bleachers where the men ate their lunch. Devon sat on the bottom step of the bleachers. Both owls flew silently over her head and vanished into the tamarisk trees that ringed the reservoir. She had often heard the owls between twilight and dawn, but this was the first time she had more than a glimpse of their faces, and it was a shock to her to discover that they didn't look like birds at all but like monkeys or ugly children, accidentally winged.

The water, which in the daytime appeared murky and hardly fit even for irrigating, shone in the moonlight as if it were clean enough to drink. She remembered a giant scoop probing the muddy depths for Robert, and bringing up old tires and wine bottles and beer cans, pieces of lumber and rusting machinery, and finally, the baby bones which Valenzuela had carried away in a shoe box. Months later she'd asked Valenzuela about the bones. He said the baby had probably been born to one of the girls who followed the migrants. Staring down at the water Devon thought of the dead child and the long-gone mother, and of Valenzuela simultaneously crossing himself and cursing as he packed the bones into the little shoe-box coffin.

Suddenly a match flared on the opposite side of the reservoir and moments later the smell of cigarette smoke floated across the water. She knew that members of the Estivar household were forbidden to smoke—"The air," Estivar said, "is already dry and hot and dirty enough"—and she was a little uneasy and more than a little curious. She rose and began moving quietly along the dusty path. She had a flashlight in her hand but there was no need to turn it on.

"Jaime?"

"Yes, ma'am."

In the moonlight Jaime's face was as ghostly white as the barn owl's. But he was neither winged nor wild and he made no attempt to escape. Instead, he took another deep drag of the cigarette, letting the smoke curl up out of his mouth and around his head like ectoplasm. Nothing materialized except a voice: "Smoke is supposed to keep the mosquitoes away."

"And does it?"

"I've only been bit twice so far." He scratched his left ankle with the toe of his right shoe. The wooden crate he was sitting on creaked rheumatically at the joints. "You going to tell my folks on me?"

"No, but they'll find out some time."

"Not tonight, anyhow. She went to bed with a head-ache and he's gone."

"Where?"

"He didn't say. He had a phone call and left the house, looking like he was glad of an excuse to get away."

"Why would that be, Jaime?"

"Him and Mom were fighting, they'd been at it ever since court."

"I didn't know your parents ever fought."

"Yes, ma'am." He took another drag on the cigarette and blew smoke, slowly and scientifically, at a mosquito that was buzzing at his forearm. "He gets mean, she gets nervous. Sometimes vice versa."

"Money," she said. "That's what most couples fight about, I suppose."

"Not them."

"No?"

"They fight about people. Us kids mostly, only like to-night it was about other people."

She realized that she shouldn't be standing in the dark prying information out of a fourteen-year-old boy but she made no move to leave or to alter the course of the conversation. It was the first time she'd ever really heard Jaime talk. He sounded cool and rational, like an elderly man assessing the problems of a pair of youngsters.

She said, "What other people?"

"Everybody whose name came up."

"Did my name come up?"

"A little bit."

"How little?"

"It was just about you and Mr. Bishop. Him and my dad don't groove, and my dad's afraid Mr. Bishop might get to be boss of the ranch some day. I mean, if he married you—"

"Yes, I see."

"But my mom says you'd never marry him on account of his *mal ojo*, evil eye."

"Do you believe in things like that?"

"I guess not. He's got funny eyes, though. Sometimes it's better not to take a chance."

"Thank you for the advice, Jaime."

"That's O.K."

The owls appeared again, flying low and in utter silence over the reservoir. One of them had a rat in its claws. The rat's tail, bright with blood, swung gently in the moonlight.

"People with *mal ojo*," Devon said, "what do they do?"

"They just look at you."

"Then what?"

"Then you got a jinx."

"Like Carla Lopez."

"Yeah, like Carla Lopez." Jaime hesitated. "She was one of the people my mom and dad were quarreling about tonight. There was a big argument over which of them hired her to work for us summer before last and which of them got the idea of hiring somebody in the first place. Mom said it was my dad's idea because Carla Lopez had worked for the Bishops the previous summer and my dad couldn't let Mr. Bishop be ahead of him like that."

"Did Carla cause any trouble when she was staying at your house?"

"Not for me. But she dangled herself in front of my brothers."

"She what?"

"Dangled herself. You know, like a drum majorette."

"I see."

"My two older brothers, both of them already had steady girl friends, so they didn't pay so much attention. But Felipe, he really twitched. So did the cop."

"What cop?"

"Valenzuela. He used to make excuses to come out to the house, things like talking to my dad about the wetback problem, but he came to see her." Jaime lowered his voice as though he suspected one of the trees might be bugged. "The word got around at school not to tangle with any of the Lopez family because they had protection. Even Felipe stayed away from them."

"Why do you say, *even* Felipe?"

"He was a good fighter, he took a mail-order course in karate. Anyway, he left at the end of summer. He didn't want to spend the rest of his life messing with fertilizers and bug sprays, so he went to find a job in the city."

This was the story Jaime had been given, and it made sense. It was also reinforced by the arrival now and then of letters which Estivar read aloud at the evening meal: *"Dear Folks, Here I am in Seattle working at an aircraft factory, making good money and feeling fine..."* Whether it was the words themselves or the slow deliberate way Estivar read them, to Jaime the letters didn't sound natural. That Felipe should write at all wasn't natural. He was too impatient. The thoughts that skittered across his mind couldn't be caught by a pen and pinned down to paper. Still, the letters came: *"Dear Folks, I won't be able to fly home for Christmas, so here is ten dollars for Jaime to buy a new sweater . . ."*

He couldn't see the expression on Devon's face but he knew she was watching him and he felt vulnerable and guilty. He wished the subject of Felipe hadn't come up. It was as if he'd been tricked into it by the night, the soft-talking woman, the reservoir catching the moon's rays like a giant *mal ojo.*

He rose abruptly, dropping the cigarette on the ground and stamping on it. "Felipe had no connection with the *viseros* that did the killing. He was gone before they were even hired. Anyway, my mom says maybe the *viseros* didn't do it, it's easy to accuse people when they aren't around to defend themselves."

Too easy, she thought. Leo's accusation that Ruth and Robert were lovers came only after they were both dead. There was no real evidence: Robert was sent away to school . . . Ruth was depressed and suffered from headaches . . . Robert didn't have girl friends . . . *"When I worked for the Bishops,"* Carla had said, *"everything was quiet. Mr. Bishop used to read a lot and Mrs. Bishop took long walks for her headaches."* What kind of walks had they been, innocent purposeless strolls around the countryside? Or did she head straight for the river, the most direct route to Robert?

"Well, I better be going," Jaime said, "before somebody comes barging out looking for me."

"Wait just a minute, Jaime."

"Sure, but—"

"I want to get in touch with Carla Lopez and I can't remember the address she gave in court this morning."

"You could ask her family in Boca de Rio, only they probably wouldn't tell you. They'd think you were trying to cause trouble for her. They're that way—you know, suspicious." After a moment he added, "I bet the cop knows where she's at—Valenzuela."

"I'll try him. Thank you, Jaime."

"You're welcome." He sounded as if he wasn't quite sure how welcome.

THERE WERE SEVERAL VALENZUELAS in the telephone directory but only one was listed in the yellow pages under Insurance. The same number was given for both office and home, and Devon had the impression of a shoe-string operation, not the kind of thing that would lure a man away from an important job in the sheriff's department.

The voice that answered the phone was hoarse and unsteady. "Hello."

"Mr. Valenzuela?"

"Who's this?"

"Mrs. Osborne. Mrs. Robert Osborne."

"If you want a policeman you called the wrong place. I'm retired. In fact, I'm tired and retired and maybe a little drunk too. How's that?"

"Not so good. I was hoping you could help me."

"I'm not in the helping business any more."

"I merely want some information," Devon said. "I thought you might know how I can get in touch with Carla Lopez."

"Why?"

"I'd like to ask her some questions."

"She has no phone."

"Can you tell me where she lives?"

"She's not home tonight."

"I see. Well, I'm sorry to have bothered you. I can get her address tomorrow morning from the court records or from Mr. Ford."

There was such a long silence that Devon thought Valenzuela had hung up or perhaps walked away from the phone to pour himself another drink. Then, "Catalpa Street. 431 Catalpa Street, Apartment 9."

"Thank you, Mr. Valenzuela."

"You're welcome."

It was the second time within the hour that she'd been welcome but not very.

CHAPTER FIFTEEN

AS SOON AS Estivar stopped the station wagon, lights went on around the outside of the house as though Mrs. Osborne had been waiting for him in the dark with the relentless patience of a predator. Fog had rolled in from the sea and the merry-go-round wind chime above the courtyard door was still. The brass horses who'd pranced and galloped all afternoon to the sound of their own music stood silent now except for the moisture dripping off their hoofs onto the flagstones below.

"You came," Mrs. Osborne said, sounding a little surprised that he'd kept his word.

"I usually obey orders, ma'am."

"It wasn't an order. Dear me, you've completely misunderstood the situation."

In her blond wig and cherry-red velvet robe she looked as though she were going to a party or expecting one to come to her. Estivar didn't feel like a party, either coming or going. The fog made him uneasy. It seemed to cut off the rest of the world and leave him alone in a small cold gray room with this woman he feared.

He said, "You sent for me."

"Of course. I thought it was time you and I had a nice friendly chat. It might be our last . . . Now, don't go imagining that I'm depressed or anything like that. I'm simply being realistic. Things do happen, you know. People go away, they die, they even become other people sometimes. Things happen," she repeated. "Come in the house, won't you?"

"All right." He was glad to get out of the fog. At least the house was warm, the lamps were lit and there was a fire glowing gold and coral in the grate.

She sat down in one of the wing chairs flanking the fireplace, motioning him to take the other. There was a backgammon table between them. The dice were thrown and the black and white pieces arranged as if someone had walked out in the middle of a game. She and Robbie used to play backgammon, Estivar thought. She always let him win even if she had to cheat to do it; so that when he lost to Rufo or Cruz he was bewildered, he couldn't understand the sudden failure of luck and skill together.

"You look nervous, Estivar," she said. "And guilty. Do you have anything to feel guilty about?"

"Nothing that would be of interest to you, ma'am."

"In your testimony this morning you made some unflattering references to my family. I don't mind for myself.

But you gave people the wrong impression of my son."

"I didn't mean to do that. I meant to give them the right impression."

She either missed the irony or pretended to. "Whatever your intentions, the effect was the same—that my son was prejudiced, that he didn't get along with his own foreman, let alone the migrant workers. It's all on the record now and there's only one way it can be removed."

"What is that?"

"It would invalidate the whole hearing if Robert were to turn up alive."

He thought of the blood in the mess hall, seeping between the cracks in the floorboards and soaking into the soft pinewood and standing in puddles as though it had dripped from a leaky roof. "Mrs. Osborne, he's not going to—"

"Stop. I refuse to listen to you. What do you know about it, anyway?"

"Nothing," he said, wishing it were true. "Nothing."

She was staring down at the backgammon board, frowning, as if the game had begun again and it was her turn. "The police will be useless from now on. The hearing gives them the excuse they've been waiting for to drop the case completely. So it's up to you and me."

"How do I come into it, Mrs. Osborne?"

"You have a great many friends."

"Some."

"And relatives."

"A few."

"I wanted you to see that they get the message as soon as possible."

"What message?"

"About the new reward. I decided to handle the details personally, without an intermediary like Mr. Ford." Ford had, in fact, refused to be a party to it or even to discuss it with her. "It's often occurred to me that the first reward was bungled. There were too many strings attached. This time I've offered to pay $10,000 for any information at all concerning my son after he left the house that night."

"You're letting yourself in for a lot of trouble."

"What have I got now? Do you think this isn't trouble, not knowing whether your only child is dead or alive? But you wouldn't understand. If something happened to Cruz, you'd still have Rufo and Felipe and Jaime and the twins. I had only Robert." She went over to the cherrywood desk and opened one of the drawers. "I was looking through some old pictures tonight and found this . . . Do you remember?"

It was a color snapshot, enlarged and framed, of a tall towheaded smiling boy in his early teens. He held a spaniel pup hardly bigger than his own hand, and the pup, too, seemed to be smiling. The picture was of youngness, boyhood and puppyhood.

"I took it the day he brought Maxie home with him," she said. "Neither Mr. Osborne nor I cared much for dogs, but Robert coaxed and made such a fuss we had to let him keep it. He adored Maxie. He thought he was the luckiest boy in the world to find a pup out on the road like that."

"He didn't find it on the road."

"It must have fallen from a passing car."

"Mrs. Bishop gave it to him."

"Robert found the dog on the road," she repeated, "and brought it to the house. Your memory isn't improving with the years, Estivar."

"No." But he knew it wasn't getting any worse either.

THE SCENE REMAINED SHARP AND CLEAR in his mind. It was late afternoon and he'd started out for the ranch house to check some bills with Mr. Osborne. The sounds of quarreling struck his ears before he got as far as the garage.

Either Mrs. Osborne hadn't had a chance to close the windows and doors as she usually did or else she no longer cared who listened and what was overheard.

"He's to return it to her," Osborne said. "Right now."

"Why?"

"The dog's obviously pure-bred and maybe pedigreed. She might have paid a hundred dollars for it, or more."

"She thinks Robbie is a fine boy and she's only showing her appreciation."

"You always take his side, don't you?"

"He's my son."

"He's mine too. But no one would ever guess it, you've made such a softie out of him. He's fifteen. When I was fifteen I was earning my own living, I had a couple of girl friends—"

"Are you saying in all seriousness that you want Robert to grow up like *you?*"

"What's the matter with me?"

"If you have plenty of time I'll tell you."

Then the piano started—"March of the Toreadors," "Onward, Christian Soldiers," the pieces she played best and loudest. When Estivar returned to his own house he found Robbie sitting on the front porch with the pup cradled in his arms. For such a young dog it was very quiet and sober, as if it sensed that its presence was causing trouble.

The boy said, "Are they fighting?"

"Yes."

"The Bishops never fight."

"How do you know that?"

"She told me. She's very nice. We both like animals a lot."

"Robbie, look. You're getting to be a big boy now and—"

"That's what she said."

The fighting went on intermittently for weeks. To the

extent that it was possible, Estivar avoided the ranch house. So did Robbie. He rose long before dawn to get his chores done early and then he went roaming around the countryside with the pup at his heels. He came back from one of these excursions with the story that his father had fallen off the tractor and was lying unconscious in a field. Mr. Osborne died five days later. He had a big funeral but no mourners . . .

"IT DOESN'T MATTER NOW where he got the dog," Estivar said. "It was a long time ago."

"And your memory has failed."

"If you say so, Mrs. Osborne."

She replaced the picture of the boy and pup in the desk drawer, handling it with care, as though it were still a negative that would vanish in the light.

"He was always doing things like that," she said, "rescuing birds that had fallen out of nests, bringing home lost dogs. That will be the worst part, really."

"What will?"

"When he comes back, telling him Maxie is dead. I dread that, I dread it terribly. I don't suppose you'd tell him for me, would you, Estivar?"

"Listen to me—"

"I'd consider it a personal favor."

For a minute the silence in the room was so complete that Estivar could hear the fog falling from the eaves. "All right," he said at last. "When he comes back I'll tell him Maxie is dead."

"Thank you. That's a load off my mind."

"You must try now to think of your *own* future, Mrs. Osborne."

"Oh, I am. In fact, I've been making plans for a trip to the Orient."

"I'm glad to hear it."

"Robert's always loved Chinese food. And of course he won't want to go back to the ranch. You can hardly blame him. He was stuck there for so many years. It's time for him to see more of life, new countries, different people."

"You're forgetting his wife."

"He has no wife. She gave away his things. That's just like a divorce. In the eyes of God it *is* a divorce. She repudiated him, she gave away nearly everything he owned, even his glasses. It was pure luck I was able to rescue them."

She went over to the picture window and stood facing it, though the drapes were drawn and there was nothing to see. Estivar noticed that one of the drapes had wrinkles and soil marks in the middle, as if it had been pushed aside dozens, perhaps hundreds, of times so that she could look out at the street. The sheer futility of it moved him to anger, compelled him to argue with her.

"You've always been a very practical woman," he said.

"If that's a compliment, thanks."

"What do you think happened the night Robert disappeared, Mrs. Osborne?"

"Many things could have happened."

"But which of them did, in your opinion?"

"My private opinion, not to be repeated to anyone?"

"Your private opinion, not to be repeated."

She turned from the window to face him. "I think they had a fight, he and Devon, and he simply walked out on her."

"That doesn't fit in with the testimony."

"What's testimony? It's only people talking. And people lie, they lie to protect themselves or to make themselves look good or for money or for any of fifty other reasons. The presence of a judge and a Bible doesn't make much difference."

"You were in court this morning, Mrs. Osborne."

"Of course I was. You saw me."

"Then you heard Robert's wife testify that when he left the house that night he was wearing his contact lenses, which were later found broken on the floor of the mess hall."

"I heard her."

"She also stated that Robert's prescription sunglasses were still in the glove compartment of his car."

"Yes."

"And you have the horn-rimmed glasses he usually wore."

"Yes."

"So you must know that Robert didn't walk out on his wife. He couldn't have gone anywhere without glasses of some kind."

A flush rose up from her neck, staining her whole face scarlet until even her eyes were bloodshot. "You're on *her* side."

"No."

"You're against me."

"I'm not. If you'll just—"

"Get out of my house."

"All right."

Neither of them spoke again. The only sound in the room was a log shifting in the grate as though it had been kicked.

CHAPTER
SIXTEEN

CATALPA STREET was in one of the city's older sections, which Devon had never seen before. Turn-of-the-century frame houses alternated with recently constructed low-rent apartment buildings.

431 was of modern design in stucco and redwood and almost new, but it was already breaking down from over-use and neglect. Most of the units had wall-to-wall children. As ceiling plaster cracked and paint peeled and plumbing wore out, no one had the interest or money or capacity to repair them. With deterioration came con-

tempt. Initials were carved in woodwork, epithets written on walls. Trees were broken off before they had a chance to grow. Outside taps leaked, forming mudholes, while a few feet away shrubs died from lack of water, shriveling in the morning sun. The whole area was landscaped with litter. Number 9, at the rear on the second story, had Carla's name on a piece of cardboard taped to the door. *C. Lopez* printed in tiny letters in pale green ink indicated that Carla wasn't particularly anxious to be found.

Devon pressed the doorbell. She couldn't be sure whether or not it was ringing inside the apartment because there was so much noise coming from below. Though it wasn't a holiday, half a dozen school-age children were playing in the service alley. Devon pressed the bell again, and when this failed to bring a response she rapped sharply with her knuckles.

"Carla? Are you in there, Carla?"

The door of the next apartment opened and a young black woman stepped out, carrying a child's teddy bear. Her eyes were weary and swollen and she held her body as if it hurt. Like the building itself she seemed to be a victim of overuse and neglect.

She said, "No," in a low-pitched hoarse voice.

Devon stared at her. "Pardon?"

"No, she ain't there. You from Welfare?"

"No."

"Lopez went off with some guy early this morning."

"What about the baby?"

"She was gonna drop it off at her mother's place and then she and the guy was gonna go away by themselves . . . You sure you ain't from Welfare?"

"I'm a friend of Carla's."

"Then you know she lost her job."

"Yes."

"She was feeling real blue about it and on top of that

she got some kind of court order. But last night I could hear her moving around in there, singing away to herself—like happy, you know? I figured she found a new job. But then she came over and told me how she was going on a vacation."

"Where?"

"Some city up North. Like way up North, out of state."

"Do you remember the name of it?"

"I never been out of state."

"Would you remember if you heard it again?"

"Maybe so."

"Seattle," Devon said.

"Seattle." The young woman passed her fingers across her mouth as though she were trying to feel the shape of the word. "Seattle, is that way, way up North?"

"About as far as you can get without leaving the country."

"That sounds like the place."

"Did you see Carla leave?"

"Couldn't help it. I was standing right where I am this minute."

"Was the man with her?"

"He waited down on the street beside the car." Her eyes fired up for a moment like pieces of coal. "Maybe the car was stolen, eh?"

"Had you ever seen the man before?"

"No. But I kind of suspicioned from the way the two of them acted that he was a relative, not a boy friend. Her uncle, maybe."

"Then he wasn't a young man?"

"No. He moved heavy."

"Uncles don't ordinarily go on vacations with nieces."

"Oh, he didn't want to go, I could tell that. He kept leaning against the car, hungover maybe, or maybe just blue. Anyhow, it was a funny scene, her flying around like a bird and him dead on his feet."

A girl flying happy like a bird, Devon thought, *and a hungover uncle dead on his feet.*

She said, "Thank you, Mrs.—"

"Harvey. Leandra Harvey."

"Thanks very much, Mrs. Harvey."

"Sure. Any time."

The two women stared at each other for a moment as if they both knew there wouldn't be another time.

DEVON STOPPED AT A GAS STATION and put in a call to Ford's office. She had to wait several minutes before Ford's voice came on the line, soft and precise: "Yes, Mrs. Osborne?"

"I'm sorry to bother you."

"No bother."

"It's about the girl who testified at the hearing yesterday morning, Carla Lopez. She has no phone and I wanted to ask her some questions, so I drove into the city to see her."

"And did you?"

"No. That's why I'm calling. The woman who lives next door told me Carla left this morning on a vacation with a man."

"Nothing illegal about that."

"I think I know who the man was and I'm pretty sure I know where they're going. There's something peculiar about it. I'm worried."

"All right, come on over to the office. I was going to get in touch with you anyway—I've had a couple of queries from Judge Gallagher. You may be able to answer them. Where are you?"

"On Bewick Avenue about three blocks from Catalpa."

"Keep heading south and you'll hit the freeway. It should take you fifteen minutes."

It took twenty. She wasn't used to California freeways, and on the other occasions when she'd gone to consult Ford someone else had driven her and she hadn't paid much attention to the route.

Everything in Ford's office had been designed to shut out the city, as if its noise might shatter a thought and its polluted air suffocate an idea. The picture window with its view of the harbor was double-plate glass, the ceiling was cork, the walls and floors were covered with thick wool. The chairs and the top of the massive desk were made of leather and even the ashtrays were of a non-resonant material, myrtle wood. The only metal in the room was the gold wedding band Ford wore to protect himself against overeager clients. He wasn't married.

"Good morning, Devon," he said. "Please sit down."

"Thanks." She sat down, a little puzzled. It was the first time he'd called her Devon. She knew it hadn't been done on impulse, that years in the practice of law had left Ford with a minimum of spontaneity. What he said and did, even the gestures he made, seemed planned for hidden judges and secluded juries.

"So Carla Lopez has gone on a vacation," he said. "Why should that bother you?"

"I'm pretty sure she went to Seattle."

"Seattle, Peoria, Walla Walla—what difference does it make?" He stopped suddenly, frowning. "Wait a minute. Someone referred to Seattle during the hearing. The Estivar boy."

"Jaime."

"As I recall, it was simply a casual remark to the effect that one of his brothers worked in Seattle and had sent him money for Christmas."

"The brother's name is Felipe and Carla had a crush on him. She still has."

"Who told you?"

"Carla herself. So did Jaime when I met him last night

at the reservoir. He said that during the summer Carla worked for his family she made a play for all the brothers. The two older ones didn't pay much attention but Felipe really twitched."

"*Twitched?*" His shock was genuine. "Where did you get—"

"That's the expression Jaime used."

"I see."

"Felipe left the ranch, and the area in general, more than a year ago."

"Before or after the girl got pregnant?"

"Oh, I think after. She's apparently been trying for a long time to get in touch with Felipe and no one would give her any information about him."

"Did Jaime tell you that, too?" Ford asked.

"No. I overheard a conversation in the hall yesterday afternoon when I went to phone Mrs. Osborne. The phone booth was stuffy and I kept the door open a little. There were two people talking just outside. One of them was Carla, the other was the policeman, Valenzuela."

"Ex-policeman."

"Ex-policeman. He said something like 'not knowing a thing about it until a few minutes ago.' But she claimed he was lying to her the way the Estivars had. He warned her to stay away from the ranch and she told him she wasn't afraid of the Estivars or the Osbornes or anyone else because she had her brothers to protect her."

"What made you jump to the conclusion that they were referring to Felipe?"

"It wasn't a very long jump. Carla had a crush on Felipe and the chances are he's the father of her child. She'd naturally be angry if someone knew where he was and refused to tell her."

"So she found out where he was and now she's going there?"

"Yes."

"With another man? That seems a bit tactless."

"Necessary, though. She doesn't have money for a trip like that. She had to talk somebody into taking her."

"And you're pretty sure of that somebody's identity?"

"Yes. It was Valenzuela."

He leaned forward in his chair and the leather made a soft patient sighing sound. "Would you like to see my file on the girl?"

"Of course."

He pressed the intercom. "Mrs. Rafael, please bring in the Carla Lopez file."

It was brief: Carla Dolores Lopez, 431 Catalpa St., Ap't. 9. Age 18. Waitress, currently unemployed. Uses her maiden name though not yet divorced. Married Ernest Valenzuela Nov. 2/67 in Boca de Rio. Gave birth, March 30/68, to male child registered as Gary Edward Valenzuela. Separated from husband July 13/68 and moved to present address in San Diego. Juvenile record for shoplifting, habitual truancy.

"The baby," Ford said, "may or may not be Valenzuela's. Under the law any child born to a married woman is presumed to have been fathered by her husband unless proven otherwise. Nobody's tried to prove otherwise. Maybe there isn't an otherwise." He turned the file face down on his desk. "If the girl left town this morning with Valenzuela, it might simply indicate a reconciliation."

"But they're heading for Seattle, where Felipe is. She couldn't very well ask her estranged husband to help her track down her former lover."

"My dear Devon, many bargains are struck in this life that you wouldn't understand or condone. The girl wanted to go to Seattle and one way or another was willing to pay for the trip."

"So you think everything is just dandy."

"I think practically nothing is just dandy. But—"

"I'm worried about Carla. She's very young and emotional."

"She's also a married woman with a child, not a runaway kid who can be picked up and held in juvenile hall for her own protection. Besides, I have no reason to believe Valenzuela poses any threat to her, or to anyone else. As far as I know, his record with the sheriff's department over the years was good."

"Mrs. Osborne told me he was incompetent."

"Mrs. Osborne thinks most people are incompetent," Ford said dryly. "Including me."

"She also told me that he didn't resign, he was fired."

"When he left the department various stories were heard around the courthouse. The official one was that he resigned to take a job with an insurance company—true as far as it went. Privately it was rumored that he'd begun to slip because of heavy drinking. His marriage didn't improve the situation. The Lopez family is large and trouble-prone and Valenzuela's connection with it was bound to cause friction in the department." He frowned up at the ceiling like an astrologer looking for stars to read. "How he got involved with the girl in the first place I wouldn't know. Affairs of the heart are not in my sphere of competence. Or interest."

"Really? You asked me enough personal questions about my life with Robert."

"Only because it was my business to present to Judge Gallagher the picture of Robert as a happily married young man."

"You sound as if you doubt that he was."

"My doubts, if any, are irrelevant. I think I've proved to the court's satisfaction that Robert is dead. Of course I won't be absolutely sure until Judge Gallagher announces his decision on the hearing."

"And when will that be?"

"I don't know yet. When he called me earlier this

morning I expected him to set a time for the announcement. Instead, he asked me some questions."

"What about?"

"First, the truck."

"The old G.M. belonging to the migrant workers?"

"No. It was the pickup Jaime referred to at the end of his testimony yesterday afternoon. I didn't pay much attention, since Jaime seemed to be merely making a passing remark. But Judge Gallagher's a stickler for details. He read that section of the transcript to me over the phone. I'll repeat it for you:

"*Q.* Jaime, do you recall anything in particular about the crew?

A. Just the old truck they came in. It was painted dark red, I noticed that specially because it was the same color red as the pickup Felipe used to teach me to drive. It's not there any more, so I guess Mr. Osborne sold it on account of its gears being stripped too often."

Devon nodded. "I remember, but why is it important?"

"Judge Gallagher wants to know what happened to the truck and where it is now."

"I can't answer that."

"Who can?"

"Estivar is responsible for all the vehicles used on the ranch. I'll ask him about it when I get home. I'm sure there's a perfectly logical explanation and that the truck had nothing to do with Robert's death."

"You'll take Estivar's word for it?"

"Of course."

He watched her carefully for any signs of doubt. There were none, and after a moment or two he continued. "Judge Gallagher is also curious about the weapon, the butterfly knife. So am I. A great deal of effort went into the disposing of the body. The knife could have been disposed of at the same time and in the same place. Instead, it was tossed into a pumpkin field. The pumpkins had been gathered for market at the beginning of October and the field was due to be cleared and plowed. Any agricultural worker would have known this."

"So the knife was meant to be found," Devon said. "Or else whoever threw it into the field was not an agricultural worker. I'm inclined to believe the first theory."

"Why?"

"Everyone in our area is connected with agriculture. Even the strangers passing through are ranch hands or migrant laborers."

"Gallagher made a further point: no poor Mexican field worker would have discarded a knife like that. He would have washed it off and kept it, no matter what it had been used for."

A sonic boom shook the building like an explosion. Ford got up and hurried over to the windows as though he hoped to catch a glimpse of the offending plane. Seeing none, he returned to his desk and made a note on his memo pad: report s. boom, 11:32. His report would be one of many, followed by an equal number of protestations of innocence from every air base within a thousand miles.

Ford said, "The real question is why the knife, if it was meant to be found, did not implicate anyone. Ownership was never proved, which would indicate either that something went wrong or that somebody did a cover-up."

"Who?"

"Valenzuela was in charge of the case. Suppose he knew who owned or had access to the knife but kept quiet about it."

"Why would he do that?"

"Let's ask him when he gets back from vacation."

"That might not be for weeks," Devon said. "Will we have to wait that long for Judge Gallagher to make his decision?"

"No. It's already been made, unofficially—he's convinced of Robert's death, and the points he raised over the telephone aren't going to affect that. But, as I told you previously, he's a stickler for details. He's also presided at a lot of murder trials, and if yesterday's hearing had been a trial, any questions about the knife and the pickup truck would have had to be considered very carefully."

"Were those the only points he brought up?"

"The only physical ones," Ford said. "The other was psychological, having to do with Estivar's testimony. You may recall that I asked Estivar how long he'd known Robert. He stated that he'd known him since birth, that as a boy Robert used to follow him around; that Robert spent a great deal of time at the Estivar house and this close relationship continued until Robert was sent away to a prep school in Arizona after the death of his father. When he returned to the ranch two years later a considerable change had occurred in him. He no longer went to the Estivar house for meals, he avoided the Estivar boys and his relationship with Estivar himself was strictly business. Estivar blamed the change on the school in Arizona, claiming it taught Robert prejudice. Judge Gallagher refuses to buy this. He contends that a boy of fifteen who'd been brought up among Mexicans, who spoke their language and shared their food, couldn't be taught prejudice against them, certainly not at that particular school."

"Why not that particular school?"

"Judge Gallagher knows a great deal about it," Ford said. "He sent his own sons there, it's a good liberal prep school. So whatever reason Robert had for avoiding the Estivars, it wasn't prejudice he'd learned at school. Naturally Gallagher is curious about what the real reason was. So am I. The question arises whether Estivar believed the story he told on the witness stand or whether he was using it as a cover-up. You might want to ask him."

"Why might I?"

"Well, you're going to be asking him about the pickup truck anyway."

"If he didn't tell the truth in court, under oath, what makes you think he'll tell it to me?"

"He probably won't. But his reaction to the question should be interesting ... I'm flying up to L.A. for a conference this afternoon and won't be back in my office until tomorrow morning. Call me then, if you have anything interesting to report."

CHAPTER
SEVENTEEN

SHE DIDN'T SEE ESTIVAR until late in the afternoon.

She was in the kitchen helping Dulzura prepare dinner when she looked out the window and saw a man walking across a tomato field. Birds rose into the air like blown leaves at his approach, and fluttered down again as he passed. Although the man was too far away to be identified by sight, Devon knew it must be Estivar because he was the only one on the ranch who walked. The others rode, they rode anything on wheels, even if they had only a hundred yards to go and nothing to carry.

As soon as Devon stepped out the back door she was trapped between the heat of the sun and the heat rising from the earth. It was like being struck by simultaneous gusts of fire from above and from below, and she stood motionless for a fraction of a minute, her breath caught in her throat. Then she started toward the field, shading her eyes with one hand. The vines had been picked, but here and there sun-baked tomatoes still hung like red balloons filled with water.

Estivar saw her coming and he took off his hat and waited. The birds swooped past him, unafraid, as if they knew he was only a scarecrow.

She said, "Have you finished work for the day?"

"Yes, Mrs. Osborne."

"You might like to come in the house for a glass of beer or iced tea."

"Has something happened?"

"No. I just want to ask you a question."

"What about?"

"One of the trucks."

"All right."

They began walking, single file, between the rows of dying plants that still smelled fresh and fruitful. When they entered the ranch house Estivar stood just inside the door, twisting his dusty straw hat in his hands and shifting his weight from one foot to another. He'd been in that house hundreds of times, yet he looked like a stranger who'd gotten into it by accident and wanted to escape.

"Come and sit down," she said. "I'll get you a drink."

"No, ma'am, I'm not thirsty. Which one of the trucks?"

"The old red pickup Jaime referred to on the stand yesterday. He said it's not in the garage any more."

"No."

"What happened to it?"

"It—I think it got wrecked."

"Who wrecked it?"

"I don't know. Probably one of my sons," he added. "They were always in a hurry."

"The vehicles on the ranch are covered by insurance, I understand."

"Yes."

"Then a claim is filed when one of them is damaged?"

"Yes."

"And there should be a record of such a claim."

"There should, yes. Why are you asking these questions?"

"Judge Gallagher called Mr. Ford to check certain points that were brought up during the hearing. He wanted to know what happened to the pickup truck."

"I see." Whatever it was he saw hurt his eyes. He rubbed them with the back of his hand. "The truck—it had nothing to do with Mr. Osborne's disappearance. It was gone before he was."

"You sounded quite vague about it a minute ago. How can you be so sure now?"

"I'm sure."

"What happened to it?"

"Felipe took it when he left the ranch. He had to move fast, people were after him."

"Who was?"

"The girl, Carla Lopez. She was pregnant and she blamed Felipe for it. She kept threatening to send her brothers to beat him up if he didn't marry her. She's a loose-living girl. I couldn't let my son be forced into marrying her when there was a good chance he had nothing to do with her pregnancy. He was only eighteen, too young to be stuck with a family and no future. I told him to take the truck and get out of here fast. It was an old truck, worth very little. I didn't think it would be missed."

A long slanting ray of sun was coming in the window at the top of the door. Inside it, particles of dust moved back and forth like a miniature mob scene caught in a spotlight. Estivar shifted position slightly, so the shaft of sun touched the side of his face and the little dustmen milled around his left eye and ear and leaped across the furrows in his cheeks.

"If you want to call it stealing—"

"No, of course not."

"—call it mine, not Felipe's. I would have stolen more than a truck to get him away from that girl."

"I think Carla's on her way to Seattle now to look for him."

"She won't find him."

"She seems very determined."

"It doesn't matter. He's not there, he never was. I made up letters once in a while for the sake of his mother and Jaime . . . No, she won't find him," he repeated, but there were echoes of sadness in his voice as if he almost wished that Felipe had stayed and married the girl and lived happily now and then.

IT WAS ABOUT EIGHT O'CLOCK when she saw Estivar's station wagon leaving the garage, its headlights prying into the darkness.

THE CAFÉ was on the main street of Boca de Rio and it was identified by a small pink neon sign as Disco's. The proprietor was a Scot named MacDougall but the Mexicans started calling him Disco when he had a juke box installed years ago, and he'd kept the name because he liked the friendly people who gave it to him.

When Estivar arrived the café was empty except for Disco himself, three men drinking beer in a booth and a pair of teen-agers sharing a bowl of chili at one end of the counter. Estivar sat down at the other end, moving slowly and cautiously as though he suspected the place was booby-trapped.

"What'll it be?" Disco said.

"Coffee and a doughnut."

"Plain or sugar?"

"Sugar."

The doughnut, served on a paper napkin, was stale and the coffee bitter with chicory. After a mouthful of each, Estivar said, "I'm looking for Ernest Valenzuela. Someone told me he hangs out here."

"He does."

"I want to ask him about an insurance policy."

"You're too late. He left town this morning, and the way I heard it, maybe he's not coming back. He kept talking about going some place and starting over but he couldn't make a move until the Osborne case was settled. He was the chief witness. He used to be a cop, did you know that?"

"Yes."

Disco leaned across the counter. "Say, you look kind of familiar to me. Did we meet somewhere, maybe a long time ago?"

"I don't think so. My name is Estivar."

"Some boys called Estivar used to come in here a lot, they worked on the Osborne ranch. Any relation to you?"

"My sons."

"Oh." Disco thought about it awhile and then added, "They were O.K."

"Yes."

"One of them was pretty scrappy—Felipe—he liked to fight with the Lopez boys. They'd go out the back door and zap each other around. It was all more or less in fun, kid stuff, until Luis Lopez started carrying a knife. Then it got serious."

"What kind of knife?"

"A fancy little hinged job, made in the Philippines, called a butterfly knife. I told Valenzuela about it, but he said forget it. So I forgot it. In a business like this you learn to forget and remember at the right times."

Estivar took a bite of the doughnut. It felt gritty between his teeth as if the grains of sugar were turning into sand.

"Now this," Disco said, "this is a pretty good time to remember—the Osborne case is over and Valenzuela's left town. And suddenly my head's clearing, know what I mean?"

"I think so."

"Not that I ever had any important information about the Osborne case, just little things. The night Osborne was killed, for instance, Luis Lopez was in here and he had a butterfly knife with him. That doesn't mean it was *the* knife, of course. Or even if it was *the* knife—well, somebody could have taken it from him. It was Friday—Friday's a big night in Boca de Rio and there were lots of people in the place, including your son, Felipe."

"You made a mistake. Not Felipe."

"I'm sure."

"Felipe was nowhere near here at that time. He'd left the ranch three weeks earlier."

"He came back."

"No. He went to Seattle, he was in Seattle working at an aircraft factory. He wrote letters. Ask my family about the letters."

"He was in here, Mr. Estivar, just as sure as you're in here yourself right now. He told me he'd run out of money and he was going out to the ranch to get some from you as soon as he could hitch a ride. I don't know what occurred after he left."

"Nothing," Estivar said. "Nothing."

"All I know is, Luis Lopez happened to walk past the place and looked in the window and saw Felipe sitting here at the counter. He came in and started an argument about his sister, Carla. Pretty soon it turned into a real fight. Luis had a bloody nose by the time I kicked both of them out on the street."

Estivar stared into the empty cup. He couldn't recall drinking the coffee or eating the doughnut, but they were both gone and a leaden lump was forming in the middle of his chest. *Luis had a bloody nose.* He knew now the source of the blood on Felipe's shirt sleeve, the type O which Ford thought indicated the presence of a third man. There weren't three men in the mess hall that night. There were only two—Robert Osborne and Felipe.

"Not that it matters," Disco said, "the Osborne case being over and Valenzuela not around, not even a cop any more. But I figure it could have happened then, if it happened at all. I mean, it's just a theory."

"What?"

"Luis drew the knife and Felipe took it away from him."

"No," Estivar said. "No."

But he was sure now that it was true and that Valenzuela kept quiet about the knife because he thought he was protecting Carla's brother. Instead, he had protected Felipe. When Valenzuela came back and found out the truth he'd be wild with rage. He'd go looking for Felipe and he'd find him. Valenzuela had been a cop, he knew all the angles, the corners, the hiding places—the bars and back alleys of L.A., the *ramerías* of Tijuana and *garitos* of Mexicali, the flyblown *fondas* of El Paso.

There was no place that Felipe would be safe.

CHAPTER
EIGHTEEN

SHE AWOKE before there were any sounds from the kitchen below. In the half-light she dressed quickly in her ranch clothes, jeans and sneakers and a cotton shirt. When she opened the drapes to crank the window shut against the coming heat, she could see Tijuana in the distance, the cathedral gradually turning from dawn-pink to day-yellow, the wooden shacks clinging grimly to the sides of the hill like starving children to a teat. She could see, too, part of Leo's ranch. Something was burning in one of the fields.

The column of smoke rose thin and gray, a signal of despair.

She left the house by the front door to avoid waking Dulzura. The tomato fields teemed with the hungry birds of morning, but on the other side of the road the mess hall and bunkhouse were empty and silent, as though no one had ever lived there and nothing had ever happened. North of the mess hall were the acres of canteloupe where the migrants were at work, bodies bent, heads lowered and hidden under identical straw hats. None of them looked up or sideways; the direction of survival was down.

Jaime was late this year in harvesting the pumpkins for Halloween and the field was strewn with big orange heads. Although no faces had yet been carved on any of them, Devon felt that they were watching her, a hundred toothed grins and sets of geometric eyes. In the sky above her a vulture circled looking for carrion. Alternately flapping and floating, he kept coming closer and closer to her as if he thought she might lead him to something dead— a small dog by the side of the road, a woman wet from the river, a young man bleeding. She turned with a little cry, half rage, half grief, and began walking rapidly back to the house.

Dulzura, barefooted, was at the work counter measuring out coffee. "Mr. Ford called," she said. "I went upstairs to get you and you were gone."

"Yes. What did he want?"

"He left two messages. I wrote them down."

The messages, printed in large careful letters, were on a sheet of paper beside the telephone: Meet Ford in court 1:30 for judge's decision. See morning paper page 4A and 7B.

Above the story on page 4 there was a picture of a car smashed beyond recognition, and another of Valenzuela in uniform, looking young and confident and amused. The account of the accident was brief:

A former deputy in the sheriff's department, Ernest Valenzuela, 41, and his estranged wife, Carla, 18, were killed in a one-car accident late yesterday afternoon a few miles north of Santa Maria. The car was travel-ing well in excess of a hundred miles an hour accord-ing to Highway Patrolman Jason Elgers, who was in pursuit. Elgers had been alerted by an attendant at a gas station in Santa Maria where Valenzuela had stopped for refueling. The attendant said he heard the couple quarreling loudly and saw a half-empty bottle of bourbon on the front seat.

The ex-deputy was killed instantly when his car smashed through a guard rail and struck a concrete abutment. Mrs. Valenzuela died en route to the hospi-tal. They leave a six-month-old son.

The other newspaper item was a box ad on page 7. It offered $10,000 reward for information on the whereabouts of Robert K. Osborne, last seen near San Diego, October 13, 1967. All replies would be kept confidential and no charges of any kind would be pressed. The numbers of a P.O. box and of Mrs. Osborne's telephone were given.

She put the paper down and said to Dulzura, "Valen-zuela is dead."

"I heard it on the radio," Dulzura said, and that was Valenzuela's epitaph as far as she was concerned.

DURING THE MORNING Devon called Leo's house half a dozen times before getting an answer at eleven o'clock when he came in from the fields for lunch. He sounded tired. Yes, he'd heard the news about Valenzuela and Carla —one of his men had told him—but he didn't know about Mrs. Osborne's advertisement or about the time set for Judge Gallagher's decision.

"One-thirty this afternoon," he said. "Do you have to be there?"

"No, but I'm going to be."

"All right, I'll pick you up—"

"No, no. I don't want you to—"

"—about twelve-fifteen. Which doesn't leave much time for arguing, does it?"

She was waiting when he drove up to the front door. Before she stepped into the car she glanced up and saw the vulture still circling in the air above the house. He was riding so high now that he looked like a black butterfly skimming a blue field.

He noticed her watching the bird and said, "Vultures are good luck."

"Why?"

"They clean up some of the mess we leave behind."

"All they mean to me is death."

Once inside the car she couldn't see the bird any more, but she had a feeling that when she returned it would be there waiting for her, like a family pet.

Leo said, "I haven't heard any details about Valenzuela's death, or Carla's."

"The newspaper called it an accident and that's how it will go down in the record books. But it won't be right. He was drinking heavily, they were quarreling, the car was going more than a hundred miles an hour—how can all that add up to an accident?"

"It can't. They just don't know what else to call it."

"It was a murder and a suicide."

"There's no proof of that," Leo said. "And no one wants proof. It's more comfortable for everyone—the law, the church, the survivors—to believe it was an act of God."

Devon thought of Carla telling the judge earnestly about her jinx—*"Like if I did a rain dance there'd be a year's drought or maybe a snowstorm"*—and of the last time she'd seen Valenzuela outside the courtroom. He was standing alone at the barred window of the alcove, somber and red-eyed. When he spoke his voice was muffled:

"*I'm sorry, Mrs. Osborne.*"

"*What about?*"

"*Everything, how it's all turned out.*"

"*Thank you.*"

"*I wanted you to know I hoped things would be different . . .*"

She realized now that he'd been talking about himself and his own life, not just about hers or Robert's.

"Devon." Leo spoke her name sharply, as though he'd said it before and she'd failed to hear it.

"Yes."

"Whenever I see you these days we're in a car or some place where I can't really look at you. And we talk about other people, not about us."

"We'd better keep it that way."

"No. I've been waiting for a long time to tell you something, but the right moment never came around and maybe it never will. So I'll tell you now."

"Please don't, Leo."

"Why not?"

"There's something I should tell you first. I won't be staying here."

"What do you mean by 'here'?"

"In this part of the country. I'm putting the ranch up for sale as soon as I can. I'm beginning to feel the way Carla did, that I have a jinx and I must get away."

"You'll come back."

"I don't think so."

"Where will you go?"

"Home." Home was where the rivers ran all year and rain was what spoiled a picnic and birds were seagulls and hummingbirds and swallows, not *gaviotas* or *chupamirtos* or *golondrinas.*

"If you change your mind," he said quietly, "you know where to find me."

HER BRIEF REAPPEARANCE in court was, as Ford had told her it would be, merely a formality, and the moment she'd been dreading for weeks came and went so fast that she hardly understood the Judge's words:

"In the matter of the petition of Devon Suellen Osborne for probate of the will of Robert Kirkpatrick Osborne, said petition is hereby granted and Devon Suellen Osborne is appointed executrix of the estate."

As she walked back out into the corridor tears welled in her eyes, not for Robert—those tears had long since been shed—but for Valenzuela and the girl with the jinx and the orphaned child.

Ford touched her briefly on the shoulder. "That's all for now, Devon. There'll be papers to sign. My secretary will send them on to you when they're ready."

"Thank you. Thank you for everything, Mr. Ford."

"By the way, you'd better call Mrs. Osborne and tell her the court's decision."

"She won't want to be told."

"She must be, though. That ad has put her in a very vulnerable position. If she knows Robert has been officially declared dead, she's not so likely to pay some con artist $10,000 for phony information."

"Mrs. Osborne has always been quite practical about money. When she buys something, she gets what she pays for."

"That's what I'm afraid of."

Devon telephoned from the same booth she'd used two days previously. This time Mrs. Osborne answered on the first ring, a sharp impatient "Hello?"

"This is Devon. I thought I'd better tell you—"

"I'm sure you mean well, Devon, but the fact is you're tying up my line and someone might be trying to reach me."

"I only wanted to—"

"I'm going to say goodbye now because I'm expecting a very important call."

"Please listen."

"Goodbye, Devon."

Mrs. Osborne hung up, hardly even conscious that she'd told a lie. She wasn't expecting the call, she'd already received it and made the necessary arrangements.

CHAPTER NINETEEN

THE NEXT STEP was to get the house ready for his arrival. He wouldn't come before dark. He was afraid to move around the city in daylight even though she'd told him no one was looking for him, no one wanted to find him. He was safe: the case was over and Valenzuela was dead. It was sheer luck that she'd chosen to buy this particular house. The California mission style suited her purpose—adobe walls as much as two feet thick, heavy tiled roof, enclosed court, and more important than anything else, iron grillwork across the windows to keep people out. Or in.

She returned to the front bedroom and her interrupted task of fixing it up. The cartons, marked Salvation Army in Devon's small square printing, were nearly all unpacked. The old map had been taped to the door: BEYOND THIS POINT ARE MONSTERS. Robert's clothes hung in the closet, his surfing posters and college pennants decorated the walls, his glasses were on the top of the bureau, the lenses carefully polished, and his boots were beside the bed as if he'd just stepped out of them. Robert had never seen this room, but it belonged to him.

When she finished unpacking the cartons she dragged them to the rear of the house and piled them on the service porch. Then she brewed some coffee and took it into the living room to wait until the sun set. She'd forgotten about lunch and when dinner time came she felt light-headed and a little dizzy, but she still wasn't hungry. She made another pot of coffee and sat for a long time listening to the little brass horses dancing in the wind and the bamboo clawing at the iron grills across the windows. At dusk she switched on all the lights in the house so that if he was outside watching he could see she was alone.

It was nearly nine o'clock when she heard the tapping at the front door. She went to open it and he was standing there as he'd been standing a hundred times in her mind throughout the day. He was thinner than she remembered, almost emaciated, as if some greedy parasite had taken up residence in his body and was intercepting his food.

She said, "I thought you might have changed your mind."

"I need the money."

"Come in."

"We can talk out here."

"It's too cold. Come in," she said again, and this time he obeyed.

He looked too tired to argue. There were dark blue semicircles under his eyes, almost the color of the work clothes he wore, and he kept sniffling and wiping his nose with his sleeve like a child with a cold. She suspected that he'd picked up a drug habit along the way, perhaps in some Mexican prison, perhaps in one of the local *barrios*. She wouldn't ask him where he'd spent the long year and what he'd done to survive. Her only questions would be important ones.

"Where is he, Felipe?"

He turned and stared at the door closing behind him as if he had a sudden impulse to pull it open and run back into the darkness.

"Don't be nervous," she said. "I promised you on the phone that I wouldn't press charges, wouldn't even tell anyone I'd seen you. All I want is the truth, the truth in exchange for the money. That's a fair bargain, isn't it?"

"I guess."

"Where is he?"

"The sea, I put him in the sea."

"Robert was a very strong swimmer. He might have—"

"No. He was dead, wrapped in blankets."

Her hands reached up and touched her face as though she could feel pieces of it loosening. "You killed him, Felipe."

"It wasn't my fault. He attacked me, he was going to murder me like he did the—"

"Then you wrapped him in blankets."

"Yes."

"Robert was a big man, you couldn't have done that by yourself." Her voice was cool and calm. "You must come and sit down quietly and tell me about it."

"We can talk here."

"I'm paying a great deal of money for this conversation.

I might as well be comfortable during the course of it. Come along."

After a moment's hesitation he followed her into the living room. She'd forgotten how short he was, hardly bigger than Robert had been at fifteen, the year he suddenly started to grow. Felipe was twenty now, it was too late for him to start growing. He would always look like a boy, a sad strange sick little boy with a ravenous appetite and poor digestion.

"Sit down, Felipe."

"No."

"Very well."

He stood in front of the fireplace, pale and tense. On the backgammon table between the two wing chairs the game was still in progress but no one had made a move for a long time. Dust covered the board, the thrown dice, the plastic players.

She saw him staring at the board. "Do you play backgammon?"

"No."

"I taught Robert the game when he was fifteen."

Backgammon wasn't the only game Robert had learned at fifteen. The others weren't so innocent, the players were real and each throw of the dice was irrevocable. During the past year she had spent whole days thinking of how differently she would handle things if she had another chance; she would protect him, keep him away from corrupters like Ruth, even if she had to lock him in his room.

She said, "Where have you been living?"

"Tijuana."

"And you saw my reward offer in the paper?"

"Yes."

"Weren't you afraid of walking into a trap by coming here tonight?"

"Some. But I figured you didn't want the police around any more than I did."

"Are you on drugs, Felipe?"

He didn't answer.

"Amphetamines?"

His eyes had begun to water and he seemed to be looking at her through little crystal balls. There was no future in any of them. "It's none of your business. All I want is to earn the money and get out of here."

"Please don't shout. I hate angry sounds. I've had to cover up so many of them. Yes, yes, I still play the piano," she said, as if he'd asked, as if he cared. "I make quite a few mistakes, but it doesn't matter because nobody hears me, and the walls are too thick . . . Why did you kill him, Felipe?"

"It wasn't my fault, none of it was my fault. I wasn't even living at the ranch when it happened. I only went back that night to try and get some money from my father. I was a little roughed up from fighting—I ran into Luis Lopez in a bar in Boca—and that put my father in a bad mood. He wouldn't give me a nickel, so I decided to go over to the mess hall and touch Lum Wing for a loan. If my father had given me some money, like he should have, I'd never have been anywhere near that mess hall, I'd never—"

"I don't want to hear your excuses. Just report what happened."

"Rob—Mr. Osborne saw the light in the mess hall and came in to investigate. He asked me what I was doing there and I told him. He said Lum Wing was asleep and I wasn't to bother him. And I said why not, money's no use to an old man like that, all he does is carry it around. Anyway, we started arguing back and forth."

"Did you ask Robert for money?"

"No more than what he owed me."

"Robert had borrowed money from you?"

"No, but he owed it to me for my loyalty. I never said a word to anybody about seeing him come in from the field right after his father's accident. He was carrying a two-by-four and it had blood on it. I had climbed up one of the date palms looking for a rat's nest and I watched him throw the two-by-four into the reservoir. I was just a kid, ten years old, but I was smart enough to keep my mouth shut." He blinked, remembering. "I was always climbing up crazy places where no one would think of looking. That's how I found out about him and Mrs. Bishop, I used to see them meet. It went on for years, until he got sick of her and she walked into the river. It was no accident, like the police claimed . . . Well, I never said a word about those things to anybody. I figured he owed me something for my loyalty."

"In other words, you tried to blackmail him."

"I asked him to pay me a debt."

"And he refused."

"He came at me, he hurt me bad. He'd have killed me if it hadn't been for the knife I took from Luis Lopez. I hardly remember the fight, except he suddenly fell on the floor and there was blood all over. I could tell he was dead. I didn't know what to do except get away from there fast. I started to run but I caught my sleeve on a yucca spike outside the door. I was trying to get loose when I looked around and saw my father. He was staring at the knife in my hand. He said, 'What have you done?' and I said I got mixed up in a fight between Mr. Osborne and one of the migrants."

"Did he believe you?"

"Yes. But he said no one else would. I had a bad reputation for fighting and Mr. Osborne was an Anglo and things would go hard for me."

"So he helped you."

"Yes. He thought we should make it look like a robbery, so he gave me Mr. Osborne's wallet and told me to throw it away like I was to throw away the knife. He brought some blankets from the bunkhouse and we wrapped Mr.

Osborne in them and put him in the back of the old red pickup. My father said no one would miss it. That was when the dog suddenly appeared. I kicked at him to make him go away and he bit me, he bit me on the leg, and when I drove off he chased the truck. I don't remember the truck hitting him."

"Did you leave the ranch before the migrants returned from Boca de Rio?"

"Yes."

"And of course it was quite simple for Estivar to handle them. He had hired them, he paid them, he gave them their orders; he spoke their language and was a member of their race. All he had to do was tell them the boss had been murdered and they'd better get out of there fast if they wanted to avoid trouble. Their papers were forged, they couldn't afford to argue, so they left."

"Yes."

"And you, Felipe, what did you do?"

"I dropped the body off the end of a pier, then I drove across the border. It was the beginning of a weekend, there were hundreds of other people waiting to cross. No one was looking for me and no one at the ranch noticed the pickup was missing. If they had, my father would have covered for me."

"I'm sure he would. Yes, Estivar is very sentimental about his sons. You can hear it in his voice when he says *my sons. My sons,* as if he were the only one who had ever had a son—" Her voice had begun to tremble and she paused for a minute to regain control. "And that's the whole story, Felipe?"

"Yes."

"It hardly seems worth all the money I offered, especially since there were two quite serious mistakes in it."

"I told you the truth. I want my money."

"Both mistakes concerned Robert. He didn't get sick of Ruth Bishop. On the contrary, they were planning to go away together. I naturally couldn't allow that. Why, she was old enough to be his mother. I ran her off the place like a stray bitch . . . The other mistake was about the two-by-four you saw Robert throw into the reservoir. It had blood on it, his father's blood, but Robert hadn't put it there. He was protecting me. We must keep the record straight."

"I want my money," he said again. "I earned it."

"And you'll get it."

"When?"

"Right now. The safe is in the front bedroom. You can open it yourself."

He shook his head. "I don't know how. I never—"

"You just turn the dial according to my instructions. Come along."

The safe was built into the floor of the bedroom closet and concealed by a rectangle of carpeting. She removed the carpeting, then stood aside while Felipe knelt in front of the safe.

"Left to three," she said. "Right to five. Left to—"

"I can't make out the numbers."

"Are you short-sighted?"

"No. It's too dark in here. I need a flashlight."

"I think you're short-sighted." She picked up Robert's horn-rimmed glasses from the bureau. "Here, you'll be able to see better with these."

"No. I don't need—"

"Try them on. You may be surprised at the difference."

"I have good eyes, I've always had good eyes."

But even while he was protesting she was putting the glasses in position on his face. They slid down past the bridge of his nose and she pushed them back in place. "There. Isn't that an improvement? Now we'll start over. Left to three. Right to five. Left to eight. Right to two."

The safe didn't open.

"Gracious, I hope I haven't forgotten the combination. Perhaps it's left to five to begin with. Try again. Don't hurry it. I can't let you rush off immediately anyway." She reached out and touched the top of his head very gently. "We haven't seen each other for a long time, son."

DURING THE NIGHT one of the neighbors woke to the sound of a piano and went to sleep again.

ABOUT
THE AUTHOR

Margaret Millar *is internationally known
as a novelist of mystery and suspense. Her books
have been widely translated in Europe, Asia and
South America.* Beast in View *was given the Edgar
Allan Poe award by her fellow Mystery Writers
of America in 1956, and the following year she
served as president of that organization. In 1965 she
received a* Los Angeles Times *Woman of the
Year award for "outstanding achievement."*

*Born in Canada, Mrs. Millar was educated
in classics at the University of Toronto. In 1938 she
married Kenneth Millar, whose books are published
under the name of Ross Macdonald.*

*In the fall of 1958 the Millars moved into a house
in a wooded canyon just outside Santa Barbara.
Here she writes for three or four hours a day and,
for relaxation, enjoys swimming, sailing, gardening and
bird-watching. Both the Millars are active conservationists
and founding members of the Santa Barbara
Audubon Society; Mrs. Millar has written a book
entitled* The Birds and the Beasts Were There.

Date Due